KILLER WINTER

By the Author

Hiding Out

Killer Winter

Visit us at www.boldstrokesbooks.com

KILLER WINTER

by

Kay Bigelow

2018

THIS TRADE PAPERBACK ORIGINAL IS PUBLISHED BY
BOLD STROKES BOOKS, INC.
P.O. BOX 249
VALLEY FALLS, NY 12185

FIRST EDITION: MARCH 2018

CREDITS
EDITORS: VICTORIA VILLASENOR AND CINDY CRESAP
PRODUCTION DESIGN: STACIA SEAMAN
COVER DESIGN BY MELODY POND

Acknowledgments

My thanks to the Bold Strokes Books team, including Sandy Lowe, Ruth Sternglantz, and Cindy Cresap, for their patience in answering my questions and their knowledge of the whys and wherefores. My thanks to Melody Pond for creating the cover I imagined. I especially want to thank my editor, Victoria, for her understanding of my genre, her astute suggestions on needed changes, and her gentle humor regarding my gaffes.

To Reddeer for her patience in listening to me go on about people, i.e., my characters, she hasn't yet met and their foibles.

CHAPTER ONE

As Lieutenant Leah Samuels approached the crime scene, she saw cops—rookies and veterans alike—throwing up in the gutters while others kept their backs to the murder scene. Leah took a second to steel herself before stepping through the electronic plyomene screen that kept nonessential personnel from entering a crime scene. That brief moment wasn't enough to keep the bile from rising in her throat as she took in the carnage before her. For a split second, she wished she'd skipped the coffee earlier and opted for something less acidic. She had to avert her eyes to keep from joining the cops throwing up in the street. When her stomach began to settle down, she focused on her surroundings. *At the rate it's snowing, we'll lose whatever evidence there is beneath three feet of snow within a few hours. The first day of 2235 isn't beginning auspiciously.*

One thing the snow and early morning darkness couldn't hide was that a slaughter had taken place. At the edge of the crime scene, Leah stopped and studied the field. At first, all she saw was blood. Without much hope of it being true, she wondered if this was someone's idea of a New Year's Eve prank. When she took a closer look, she understood why the cops had been throwing up. Spread across the field were hundreds, if not thousands, of bits of flesh, bones, and, probably, internal organs. There was no way what she was seeing could all belong to a single person. It would take the Murder Scene Investigation team an eternity to determine the identities of the victims unless she and her team caught a huge break somewhere along the way.

What were the victims doing in a park in the middle of a blizzard? How many were here? What the phuc happened here? Who were these people and why were they killed? And why here?

Leah shuddered as another strong blast of Arctic air roared across the field. The wind and the twenty-five-below-zero cold added to everyone's misery. The conditions and the Klieg lights set up around the small field somehow added to the eeriness and horror of the site. Leah hoped they could get the evidence gathered up and into the lab before it was impossible to process.

The MSIs were dissecting the field into a grid. As each of the grid squares was set, other techs moved into the roped-off area and rapidly began shoveling as many of the small bits of flesh and bone chips as they could into evidence bags. She saw they were marking the bags with the number of the grid where the evidence was found. It appeared Dr. Scott, chief of the MSI department, had called out his entire department to help gather evidence.

There was a flurry of activity around Scott. As Leah neared the small circle of people surrounding him, she heard him tell them the weather was about to worsen. A second front was moving in and was predicted to dump an additional two or three feet of snow over the next twenty-four hours. The people around Scott cursed and began blowing whistles and waving their teams to them. As the MSIs returned to gathering evidence, they were no longer picking up everything within a grid square. They were only picking up the larger pieces of evidence from each grid. If time and weather allowed, they'd go back for the smaller pieces.

While she watched the MSIs work, Leah wished she'd ignored her wife, Quinn, and stayed in bed when the call to this scene had come in. It was supposed to be Leah's first day off in months. Quinn knew she hadn't slept through the night in weeks. *Dammit, I need today off instead of standing at the edge of this carnage.* Quinn had insisted she'd like herself better if she responded to the dispatcher. As she stood watching the techs picking up bits and pieces of her murder victims, she decided Quinn had been very wrong.

Leah looked around, trying to find her team among the growing crowd of cops who were wrapped from head to foot in bulky winter clothing. Everyone had their hoods pulled up and sitting low on their foreheads, and they had scarves wrapped around their necks and pulled up to cover their noses and chins to prevent frostbite. Everyone, herself included, looked like rotund masked bandits. The clothing made identification of individuals impossible. Leah recognized a latecomer to the scene, though. It was Weston, a member of her team. Weston swore he never used his hood because it was, he said, "girly" to do so, and he thought it a matter of male pride not to wear a scarf like "a sissy." On this morning, however, not only did he have a scarf pulled up over the lower half of his face, but he had his hood up as well. In spite of the hood, he hadn't removed the fedora he wore when out of doors regardless of the weather, making identifying him easy. The person arriving with him had to be Allison Davidson, his partner.

"Lieutenant," one of the uniforms said, interrupting her thoughts. "Dr. Scott says he's ready to begin transporting the remains."

"Thanks. Ask him to notify me when he has something."

"Yes, ma'am."

"What do you think happened here, Lieutenant?" Peony Fong asked as she came to stand with Leah. She'd lowered the scarf covering her lower face only long enough to ask the question. Leah knew she'd soon learn not to do that in this kind of weather.

Peony was a new detective, both in years and experience, with little fieldwork under her belt. She'd only been on Leah's team for a month. Leah suspected Peony had been one of the cops standing in the shadows near the street vomiting into the gutter.

The rest of Leah's team gathered around her, and Leah noticed Weston was taking his time coming to join the circle around her. She started without him.

"I don't know what happened here. Nor do I want us speculating about it until the MSIs give us some hard facts to go on." Leah didn't bother lowering her scarf. Long experience told her she'd be heard.

"Have you ever seen anything like this?" Davidson asked.

Leah shook her head. "Who's going to stay at the scene to see if there's any information to be had?" she asked.

No one volunteered, but they all looked at Peony. As the newest member of the team, she was expected to catch these kinds of assignments, and any others the rest of the team didn't want to do. Leah knew the youngster had taken each assignment as it was handed to her without complaining.

"Peony has taken the watch for the last month. I think it's time to start back at the top of the list."

"No!" Weston all but shouted. "Doesn't seniority count for anything anymore?"

"Not on my team," Leah said. "And not on this night."

"Well, it should," Weston said, narrowing his eyes as if that would intimidate Leah and make her change her mind.

Leah almost laughed out loud at the look of relief on Peony's face when she realized she wasn't going to have to stand around in the freezing cold waiting for the crime scene team to finish their work.

"I'll meet the rest of you back at the office in twenty. Peony, ride with me."

"Yes, ma'am."

Someone, almost assuredly Weston, made sucking sounds to indicate Peony was sucking up. Leah was tired of Weston and relieved that a decision had finally been made about him by the captain.

Leah led Peony to where she'd parked her car. She punched in her code and the driver's door slid open. She got in and hit the button unlocking the passenger side door. Peony wasted no time getting in and hunkering down.

Leah started the car and let it idle while the engine and the interior warmed up to freezing. She could hear Peony's teeth chattering, and she noticed for the first time Peony didn't have a winter coat on. What she had done to protect herself from the below-freezing temperatures was to add layers, lots of them. The kid looked like everyone else but only because she must have a dozen layers of sweaters on. For no particular reason, Leah flashed back to the fat cat she'd had as a child that had needed a bath. Beneath all the fur, the cat was as skinny as a rail and madder than hell at being wet.

"Where's your coat? You'll catch pneumonia if you don't wear it in this weather," Leah said as she brought herself back to the present.

"Don't own one."

"How can you not own a coat?"

"I'm not from here."

"Where are you from?"

"Xing," Peony said, naming a planet known for its year-round temperate weather and beauty. Xing had been terraformed by humans a century earlier and colonized by humans from New America.

Leah looked closer at Peony and saw she had the exotic looks of a Xing native. Unlike other women from her planet, though, Peony kept her thick hair cut short, but like her countrywomen, it was the deep rich black of a Sirulian panther. Her skin tone was a warm caramel color. Her almond-shaped eyes were so dark her pupils couldn't be seen.

"Well, get a coat, then," Leah growled.

"No money till payday."

"Drust!" Leah swore. "I think I have a spare in the office you can borrow until payday."

"No, thanks."

"What?" Leah asked, surprised at being turned down.

"Look, Lieutenant, the guys make fun of me enough as it is. I mean, my name alone was fodder for their jokes since I first walked in the door. You heard the sucking sounds when you told me to ride with you. What do you think they'll do if they find out I'm wearing the boss's coat? No, thanks. I'll just add a couple more layers of sweaters and pants."

"Who's going to tell them you're wearing my coat?"

"They'll find out. They always do," Peony said, turning away from Leah to look out the window.

"If they ask, tell them your roommate lent it to you."

"My roommate is a guy, a cop from the Twenty-seventh. Some of the guys here know Tommy. They'd just call and ask him if it's his. Besides, his coat would drag on the ground and your coat won't, and that's how they'd know."

Leah shook her head. Sometimes pride was an awful thing. "Suit yourself, Peony. But the offer stands."

"Thanks, boss."

Leah's phone rang. It was the chief MSI.

"I've released Weston and Davidson. With the amount of snow falling, there's nothing more we're going to be able to find here. Any evidence is going to have to come from forensics. We've taken hundreds of photos, videoed the scene from two different angles, and picked up evidence from every grid. We'll vacuum the scene tonight before we leave. But we started losing evidence when it hit the ground. It would still have been body temperature and would have melted through the snow. Tonight, though, we'll start trying to determine who we've got here once we get everything back to the lab. We'll keep the perimeter barriers up so when, or if, spring ever gets here, we'll come back and see what we can find."

"Thanks, Scotty, for the heads-up," she said and broke the connection.

When the car's computer told her the engine was warm enough, Leah took off. She had them in the tertiary lanes moments later.

"Why does everyone insist on driving so far off the ground here?" Peony asked as she clutched the handle above her head so hard her knuckles were white.

"I don't know what it's like on Xing, but here the primary lane is for delivery trucks and the like. The secondary lane is reserved for taxis and small busses, while the tertiary lane is for emergency vehicles and cops. The lanes above that are for personal cars. Being in the tertiary lane is much faster than in either of the lower lanes or the lanes above us," Leah told her. "Besides, we're only sixty feet off the ground."

"Isn't it better to get to your destination alive?"

Leah laughed. "I haven't killed anyone yet."

"I don't want to be the first."

"Trust me, I'll get you to the cop shop alive and in one piece."

To prove her point, she hit the accelerator and had Peony pinned to the seat for the rest of the short trip.

When they squealed into Leah's parking space and stopped only inches from the steel post at the top of the space, she glanced at Peony. Her eyes were squeezed tightly shut and her face was as white as her knuckles. Peony couldn't seem to let go of the handle. *At least her teeth have stopped chattering. Of course, she's clamped her jaw closed so tight, she might have broken some teeth. I need to take it easy on the kid.*

The "rookie ride" in her car had started many years earlier when Weston had first been assigned to her team despite her objections. She had made him ride with her to try to get him to stop being such an ass to the younger members of the team, but ended up with her being frustrated by his sense of entitlement because of his years on the force. So she gave him a ride. After that, it became a rite of passage, an initiation, for the new detectives assigned to the team. She'd tried to stop having to do it, but the detectives in the squad insisted she had to do it since they'd been put through having to ride with her.

Leah spent a few minutes at the rear of her car with the trunk open to give Peony time to recover. When Peony finally emerged from the vehicle, she still looked shaky. Leah didn't comment on how long it had taken her to get out of the car. She didn't want to add to the embarrassment the young woman must already be feeling. Neither of them said anything as they rode the glides to the third floor.

By the time they reached the offices assigned to Leah and her team, Peony looked recovered from their ride together. The kid had no way of knowing all the detectives had been in the same passenger seat, and they'd all had nearly the same reaction, and a few of them, including Weston, had thrown up after leaving her car.

From the door to her office, Leah watched as Peony entered the bullpen. The guys surrounded her and told her she'd passed the initiation of having to ride with Leah. She was now a full member of the detective squad. Peony grinned as each detective shook her hand.

Leah smiled at Peony's reaction. She knew that would help her feel more at ease with the other detectives and a lot of the ribbing and joking would end. She took off her layers of outerwear and hung them on the back of the door. She released her bootstraps and stepped out of them. She'd put on the pair of soft black leather boots she kept in her office after her feet thawed out. After she removed her hat, she finger-combed her short auburn hair to get rid of some of the results of hat hair.

She paused long enough to turn on the space heater beneath her desk, and with a deep sigh, sat in her chair and stretched her feet toward the little heater.

As she was beginning to feel her toes again, she glanced out the window that looked into the detectives' bullpen. It was made from privacy glass, allowing her to watch her detectives but not allowing them to see her. Leah noted everyone was present except Weston and Davidson. It was yet another instance of his insubordination, and she was finally going to be able to put a stop to it.

Twenty minutes later, she watched as the absent detectives strolled into the bullpen and went to their desks. Clearly, they hadn't come straight to the cop shop.

"Davidson, in my office," Leah said when the detective answered her phone.

"Yes, ma'am."

Before Davidson could take a step away from her desk, Weston grabbed her arm. She tried to jerk her arm away from him, but he had an iron grip on her wrist. Obviously, Weston wanted to know where she was going and why. Davidson finally got away from him, and a minute later, there was a knock on the door.

"Come in," Leah said.

Both Davidson and Weston walked in.

"I didn't call you, Weston."

"If you're going to talk to my partner, you may as well tell me at the same time because she'll tell me later."

"Get out."

"But—"

"You have thirty seconds to get out of my office."

"Or what?" Weston asked with a sneer.

Leah was sick and tired of his insubordination. She held his gaze but didn't respond.

Weston blinked first. "Who needs this bullshit?" He stormed out of her office, slamming the door hard enough to rattle the windows.

Leah would deal with him later. "Allison, Peony needs a partner and a mentor. She needs someone with the knowledge of how to be a good detective and how to survive the bullpen. I'd like that person to be you, if you're willing."

The relief on Allison's face was far too obvious.

"Thank you, ma'am. I'd like to work with the kid. From what I've seen, she has good instincts and the potential to be a good detective."

"I agree. Thanks for taking her on," Leah said.

"No problem."

"Where were you and Weston?"

"Ma'am?" Allison asked, clearly trying to stall for time to think of a plausible excuse.

"You heard the question. You guys got back nearly an hour after the rest of us."

"You told Weston to stay at the scene."

"I didn't say anything about you staying." Leah watched as expressions flitted across Davidson's face. She'd been a cop long enough to know when someone wasn't telling her the whole truth.

"I rode to the scene with him. He wouldn't give me the keys to the car."

"Dr. Scott released you long ago. So where have you two been?"

"Weston wanted to have breakfast," Davidson said, not able to meet Leah's eyes.

Leah watched as the young detective clenched her jaw several times. *Is she afraid of Weston? I'll kill the son of a bitch if he laid a hand on her.* "Didn't you hear me tell the team to be here in twenty?"

"Yeah. But Weston didn't care."

"Send him in when you go back out there," Leah said.

Leah saw Davidson stop by Weston's desk. As she spoke to him, she nodded in the direction of Leah's office. Weston kept Leah waiting fifteen minutes. Then he entered her office without knocking. *This is going to be fun.*

"Sit down, Weston."

"I'll stand," he said as he squared his body and looked at her defiantly.

Leah took a moment to look Weston over and didn't like what she saw. He was greasy looking—his hair was dirty, his tie had stains on it, and his shirt looked like he'd had it on for weeks. He looked like he hadn't had a shower since last fall, and she could smell him from where she sat three feet away. He was a study in brown: brown hair, brown eyes, brown suit, but then there were the black shoes and white socks. Worse than his lack of sartorial sense was that he always reminded Leah of Billy Tompkins, her grade school's resident bully. Not in looks, but in his actions. When young cops joined her team, they always looked up to Weston because of his years on the force. It didn't take them long, however, to lose their hero worship. Weston thought work was beneath him, so he had the young cops write his reports, perform the scut work of the day-to-day investigations, and never gave them credit when they solved a case for him. Everyone who had ever worked as his partner had asked for either a new partner or a transfer to another precinct within a month of being forced to work for him. He was universally hated by all, including Leah. Weston was vicious and vindictive. He'd been brought up on charges numerous times, including charges of abusing suspects more than once, but nothing had ever stuck.

"Suit yourself. I'll make this short and sweet. You're being transferred."

"What? You can't do that," he told her, clearly surprised at her news.

"It's done. I'd prefer to fire your lazy ass, but the captain said the Eighty-sixth was shorthanded, so that's where you're going."

"You can't send me out there."

"I repeat, it's done," Leah said, glad to be rid of him.

The Eighty-sixth Precinct was the armpit of the police department. It seemed like every misfit, malcontent, and suspected dirty cop was sent to the Eighty-sixth. They were always shorthanded because members of the precinct were killed on a regular basis. An internal analysis by the police commissioner's office said the high mortality rate among the cops at the Eighty-sixth was due to their own negligence. In fact, cops there were as likely to be killed by a fellow cop as by criminals.

"I'll go to the captain. He won't let you do this to me."

"Go. He signed the transfer order."

"That's where the losers go." Weston stepped toward her and glowered at her as if to intimidate her.

"You'll be amongst your own, then. Pack up your desk and be out of here in the next fifteen minutes. If you're not, I'll have you escorted out."

"You'll be sorry that you did this, bitch."

"Yeah, yeah. Get out."

They'd been at odds with one another since they'd been at the academy nearly twenty years earlier. He'd been lazy then, too. At the time, she'd been sure he'd cheated on the tests, but she couldn't prove it. He'd intimidated the weaker cadets into doing his bidding, proving he was a schoolyard bully who had simply grown older. He'd graduated last in their class. How he'd ever passed the test to get his detective's shield was beyond Leah. She was convinced it had involved bribes, or cheating, or both.

Things hadn't improved over the years. Every time Leah had been promoted, Weston went ballistic and, more than once, accused her of sleeping with the captain to get the promotion he'd believed should have been his. He'd never been promoted above detective third grade, the lowest of the detective levels. Leah didn't understand why he hadn't been fired. It was rumored he had something on the chief.

As Weston left her office, he slammed the door again, but it lacked the force of his first exit. He returned to his desk and Leah could see, but not hear, him ranting. The cops in the bullpen ignored him. He had no friends out there. Leah watched as Weston sat at his desk, leaned back in his chair, and put his feet on his desk.

Leah called the desk sergeant, Derek Kendrick. "Sergeant, Weston has been relieved of his duties here, and he's been told to leave the building within fifteen minutes. Please have some of your men up here in sixteen minutes to escort him out if he hasn't left."

"Yes, ma'am. With pleasure."

Weston stayed seated at his desk, glowering at her window, until Sergeant Kendrick and four burly cops walked in. Weston literally jumped to his feet, regained his bravado, and sauntered out of the room. He hadn't bothered to pack up his desk. While Leah was sure there was nothing in his desk but candy and gum wrappers, she'd have Davidson go through it and box up anything of importance and toss the rest into the recycler.

Leah was relieved that Weston hadn't turned violent. She was also relieved he was out of her life. She'd fought against his being assigned to her squad but had lost that battle. Now he was no longer her problem and she wouldn't have to deal with the daily complaints from her own squad members and others in the precinct house. She wasn't one to back down from a fight, but that didn't mean she enjoyed meaningless confrontations either.

Later in the afternoon, Leah received a call from Dr. Scott. "We've run an analysis on the crime scene photographs and video, and we don't think there's more than twenty victims despite the amount of blood and other evidence. We do have a tentative identification of one of the victims," Scotty said.

"Only one, and that's tentative?" Leah asked, disappointed.

"Yeah. Honestly, we may never identify the others because it looks like the evidence may be cross contaminated. If we could find teeth or fingers, we'd be able to identify more of the victims."

"Okay. Tell me what you found."

"As you know, we've found lumps of flesh all over the field, most of them tiny. When we vacuumed the field, we found hundreds of thousands of tiny bone fragments. It could take us years to identify them. Then we got lucky, we thought, when I found the partial remains of a thumb, or at least the fleshy section below the thumb." Scotty paused.

"That's good, right?" Leah asked. Even one lead could mean a break in the case.

"I couldn't get a decent print off the lump of flesh, so I ran a quick DNA scan on it. We have a preliminary identity." Scotty paused again.

"Scotty, will you give me the bottom line here?" Leah asked, getting frustrated.

"I ran the DNA test three times…"

"Drude, Scotty. Who is this person?"

"You're not going to believe this."

Leah pinched the bridge of her nose and closed her eyes in an effort to keep her temper in check. "Just tell me."

"The DNA says the hand belongs to Bishop Solomon Cohane."

Good Lord. "Bishop Cohane? *The* Bishop Cohane?" She knew Scotty wasn't the type to kid about his evidence. But this? She wished there was a way to reset the day so she could ignore the dispatcher's midnight call.

"Yes."

Cohane was the head of the planet's Christian church. He was well respected by everyone. He had a worldwide reputation for piety, for many, many good deeds, and a commitment to both his and others' religions.

"My God, what was he doing there?"

"That's your job to figure that out. Mine was to identify him."

What the phuc was the bishop doing in that field at midnight in the middle of a blizzard? The man had to be in his eighties. What or who would have lured him out on such a night? Leah tried to keep an open mind about how the bishop got to the field. *Was he killed elsewhere and his body dumped in the field? That would make as much sense as his having been lured to the field only to be killed.*

Leah tuned back into what Scotty was saying.

"We'll keep testing what we've found out there."

"Thanks, Scotty. Don't let anyone else work on this case but yourself, okay? I don't want this to hit the media until we've put together what happened in that field and why."

"I agree. My techs are cataloging what we found out there.

You and I are the only ones with this information. I'll call you later when, or if, something else turns up."

Leah thumbed off her phone, leaned back in her chair, and closed her eyes. She should be used to cases with unexpected twists, but there was no way she'd ever expected what was coming at her now.

CHAPTER TWO

L eah sat mulling over what Scotty had told her. She knew she was sitting on a time bomb and had to find a way to get off the bomb before it either derailed her career or killed it altogether. The death of the much-beloved bishop would explode in the media, and demands for the PD to find his killer would escalate every day thereafter. She and her team would be in a fishbowl with everyone watching their every move, second-guessing every decision, and demanding both her removal from the case and her resignation if she didn't find the killer fast enough for them. After a few minutes, she called Allison Davidson.

"In my office, and bring Peony with you."

"Yes, ma'am," Allison said.

The two detectives walked into Leah's office a moment later.

"Scotty has found evidence that Bishop Cohane was murdered at the killing field. Call his people and see if he's gone missing again. Don't tell them anything about him being dead. We need to keep that under wraps as long as possible. Understand?" Leah knew as the bishop aged, he'd developed a tendency to get lost if he was on his own. Each time, the police would be called and sent out to find him. Perhaps he'd been in the wrong place at the wrong time.

"Yes, ma'am," they said almost in unison.

"Allison, has Weston left the building?" Leah asked.

"Yes, ma'am."

"Boss, I'd watch your back. He said you'd pay big-time for sending him out to the Eighty-sixth," Peony said.

"Thanks for the heads-up," Leah said, not for a moment believing Weston would have the balls to come after her. She'd been threatened before by men far more dangerous than Weston, and she knew he was no more than a bullying ass.

Allison was back at Leah's door fifteen minutes later.

"I found him," she said. "Kind of."

"Alive?" Leah asked hopefully.

"No. Well, he might be. His housekeeper reported him missing this morning. She said the last time she saw him was yesterday morning when he left for his office at Saint Mike's Cathedral."

"Who caught the case?" Leah asked.

"O'Donnell at the Seventy-third," Allison said.

"I'll ask that the case be assigned to us," Leah said, not wanting to have another precinct digging around the perimeters of her case.

Leah had a bad feeling about this. She went to stand in front of what she called her murder board. The department wouldn't spring for a holographic board, citing budget constraints as the reason. She had the next best thing, though—an electronic murder board that could be projected onto a wall. It was how she kept track of her current cases. She opened a new file for this case. As the case progressed, she'd put everything related to it on the board. It was blank for now, but it would soon hold case notes, photos, interviews, and anything else she could think to put there. It helped her keep track of the minutiae every case generated and kept anything from falling through the cracks. Members of her squad had joked about her obsession with the details when she first started using the murder board technology, but when one of those details helped them solve a serial killer case a few years earlier, they stopped teasing her. She couldn't remember a time when she hadn't been fascinated by details.

She took the keyboard from the cradle and typed in when she'd caught the case, her impressions of the crime scene, what Scotty had reported about Bishop Cohane, and what Allison had found about whether the bishop was merely lost or really missing. She tried to think if she could add anything else, but nothing came to mind.

As she sat staring at the limited information she had on the case, she picked up her phone and called the captain's office.

"Franklin," the gruff voice said.

"Captain, it's Samuels. I'd like to brief you on the case we caught this morning."

"What's wrong with the old-fashioned way of briefing me? Why can't you send me your case notes?"

"The case involves Bishop Cohane."

There was silence on the other end for a moment. "Please tell me that the bishop took another wrong turn on his way home last night."

"I wish I could."

"Get up here."

Before leaving her office, Leah turned off her murder board and engaged both the encrypted password and palm print protections. She also locked her office door, something she rarely did. She took the glide up to the fifth floor and waited until the secretary, Sylvia, told the captain she'd arrived. As she waited for permission to enter the captain's office, she casually studied Sylvia. The woman had been every captain's secretary for as long as Leah could remember. She was older now, neatly dressed with her graying hair kept under control in a bun at the back of her head. She looked more like a grandmother every time Leah saw her. *Of course, I'm not getting any younger either.*

She was jerked out of her thoughts when she heard Sylvia say, "Go right in, Lieutenant."

"Thanks."

Leah had no sooner closed the door than the captain started in. "What's going on with Cohane?"

Leah didn't ask how much he knew about her case. She knew he'd always had his ways of finding things out. She wouldn't be surprised if he knew nearly as much right now as she did.

"We think he's dead."

"Think? What does the crime lab say?" the captain asked.

"Dr. Scott is unwilling to state with one hundred percent certainty that Cohane is dead." Leah wished she had better news.

"Why not?"

"The crime scene was a bloodbath. There were lumps of flesh and tiny bone fragments strewn over the entire field. Dr. Scott started testing a partial thumb in the hopes of identifying one victim. The other blood, lumps of flesh, and bone fragments will take longer to test, although he thinks there aren't more than twenty victims in total. He's facing an uphill battle on identification not only because most of the evidence in the field is no larger than a computer chip but because the blood was diluted by the amount of snow that fell between the commission of the murders and when he was able to vacuum it up."

"Good God. What happened out there?" the captain asked, rubbing his fingertips across his forehead as if wanting to chase away the implications of the victim being the bishop.

"We have no idea yet. My team can't do much until Dr. Scott figures out a way to identify who or what we're looking for. He did give me the heads-up when the thumb came up as belonging to Cohane, but he's unwilling to say unequivocally the victim *is* Cohane because of the cross contamination of the evidence."

"Has anyone contacted the bishop's office?"

"Yeah, he was reported missing this morning by his housekeeper."

"Who caught it?"

"O'Donnell at the Seventy-third."

"I'll have him transfer the case to you. They're overwhelmed with a series of home invasions and the murder of the occupants. He'll be glad to get rid of a missing persons case."

"Thanks."

"I'm assuming we have no idea what Cohane was doing there?"

"None." Leah paused, not sure what to say next.

"Well, phuc," he said as he fiddled with a small trophy he kept on his desk.

She was sure he'd immediately jumped to what a public relations nightmare this case could turn into, just as she had. It could be a career ender for both of them.

"Okay. Keep this under wraps. I don't want anything about this case leaking to the media, understand?"

"I'll put one team on it and have the others working on cases they're already in the middle of. I'll send my reports to you 'Eyes Only.' That'll help."

"Don't put any of your cowboys on this one."

"I have Allison Davidson and her partner, Peony Fong, on it. They're both sane and sensible investigators." *At least I hope they are. Fong is too new to know for sure.*

"Who's Fong?" the captain asked.

"The new kid. She's a newly minted detective. She'll replace Weston as Davidson's partner."

"You took care of him this morning?" he asked.

Leah thought he sounded as relieved as she was Weston was out of their hair. "Yeah, he's gone."

"Did he threaten you?"

Leah smothered a smile. The captain occasionally sounded like her dad when she'd been a kid and someone picked on her.

"Of course."

"Watch your back, Leah. He's a nasty piece of crud who's hated you for years. This may be the blow that throws him over the edge."

"I know. I'll be careful."

"Keep me informed."

"Yes, sir."

Leah left the captain's office and returned to her own. Her computer was dinging softly, indicating she had messages. One was from Scotty. He'd sent the crime scene photos to her.

She brought them up. There wasn't much to be seen from the photos. Eventually, she'd blow them up to see what she could see about the scene. She accessed her murder board again and stored the crime scene photos there.

A second message was from Davidson, who'd sent Bishop Cohane's driver's license to her. Leah stored it on the murder wall as well.

There was a soft knock on her door.

"Enter."

"We're assuming we need to keep this case to ourselves until further notice. How are we supposed to do that out there in the bullpen?" Peony asked when she and Davidson came in. "The guys are already wanting to know what we're up to. I've caught Thompson trying to look at what's on my computer screen. I'm pretty sure he heard a part of my conversation with the bishop's housekeeper."

Leah waved them to the chairs in front of her desk and said, "Good question. Let me figure out an answer for you." She gave them what she hoped was a reassuring smile, but by their expressions, she guessed it hadn't worked.

After Leah dismissed them, she sat at her desk thinking. *It wouldn't do much good to go door to door asking if anyone heard or saw anything. Idiots were shooting guns into the air, there were firecrackers, and the elders were probably already in bed and asleep.* What was the bishop doing there, and who were the other victims? What was the connection between an elderly religious man and the other victims? What should the logical next step be? Was there a logical next step?

While she was pondering the escalating questions, she called the captain. When he answered, she said, "I have to move this investigation off-site if there's to be any hope of containing it."

"I agree. Do you have any idea where you want to go?"

"Yeah. I have a place in mind, but I need to confirm its availability."

"Let me know."

"Yes, sir."

Leah's next phone call was to her wife.

"What an unexpected surprise, Lieutenant," Quinn said when she heard her voice. "I didn't expect to hear from you until very late tonight."

"Something unusual has come up. Can we share dinner together tonight?"

"Yet another unexpected pleasure. Where would you like to go?"

"Somewhere secure."

There was silence on the other end, and Leah knew Quinn was absorbing the request for privacy and putting two and two together. Quinn knew she'd been called out to a homicide in the early hours of the morning and now, just over twelve hours later, Leah was asking for a meeting somewhere private. Quinn had to know the case had become both sensitive and high profile.

"I'll meet you at seven at the Mexican joint."

The Mexican joint was a tiny restaurant they had started going to years before when they first began dating. Then, there had been only a tiny dining room and the kitchen. The dining room had only a half dozen tables, and the patrons could hear everything the chef said and every dropped utensil, but the aromas emanating from the tiny kitchen had been divine. Now it had evolved into a grown-up restaurant with dozens of tables and a separate bar, and even had three privacy booths.

"I'll be there." Leah allowed herself a smile of anticipation at seeing her wife, a prospect that always made the most gruesome day seem a little less ominous and overwhelming.

CHAPTER THREE

A t the restaurant, Leah waited for the maître d' to return from seating a couple. She glanced at the mirror behind the bar as she removed her hat. Her hair was standing up like she'd stuck a finger in an electrical outlet. She did a quick pat down to try to tame it before seeing Quinn. The pat down had only made matters worse. What she needed, she decided, was a haircut.

"Lootennent, it's been a long time," Jorge, the maître d' of Mama's Mexican, told her as he returned to his station.

"Too long, Jorge."

"How many will be eating with you tonight?"

"One other. We'd like a secure booth."

"Absolutely." He led the way away from the line that had formed behind Leah and through the restaurant to a row of booths surrounded by privacy panes.

"I'll send your waiter over immediately," Jorge said with a little bow.

Leah wasn't surprised to see Quinn already in the booth when Jorge opened the door for her. Jorge was the soul of discretion, and he took his job very seriously. He obviously hadn't wanted to let a random listener know Leah's dinner companion had already arrived. After taking her coat off, she slid into the booth and looked at her wife. When they'd met, she had no idea how old Quinn was, thanks to the way her kind aged. Her blond good looks kept her as youthful looking as the day they'd met. When they had first gotten together, Leah used to sit and watch her, mesmerized by her beauty. She still thought her incredibly handsome, and it made her heart sing to know Quinn loved her.

Quinn kissed her hello. "This must be some serious business if we're meeting here," she said.

"It is more than just a little serious, hon."

"What can you tell me?"

"The case I caught this morning was a bloodbath. On my way over here, Scotty called. He thinks the victims were slaughtered and shredded in an open field during the night." Leah was having a hard time getting her head around Scotty's characterization of the victims being shredded—it made the murders more horrific somehow.

"He thinks? Shredded?" Quinn looked as horrified as Leah felt.

"We have some lumps of flesh, and he's found a ton of bone fragments. Most of them aren't big enough for immediate positive identity purposes. The blood is so mixed together and diluted by the snow that it will take months, if not longer, to distinguish individuals' blood."

"It sounds horrific, and I'm pretty sure you've cleaned it up for me."

"The scene had veteran cops puking in the street."

"What haven't you told me?"

Quinn knew her too well. She paused before telling her the rest of the story. She knew she could trust Quinn implicitly. Quinn knew the importance of keeping what she told her to herself. She'd never betrayed her confidences in the years they'd been together. She took a deep breath and let it out slowly.

"This is strictly between you and me. Got it?" Leah said.

"Of course, babe. I know the rules by now."

She gave Quinn a sanitized version of what they'd found out so far.

"You have a serious problem if you have that many dead

people and no way of knowing who they are or why they're dead. No wonder we're meeting here."

There was a discreet tap on the door. Quinn pressed the button to unlock the door to the waiter.

After they ordered, they returned to Leah's case.

"Is there any way you can walk away from this?" Quinn asked.

"No."

"You know people will be gunning for you when this hits the news outlets."

"We're going to try to keep it under wraps until we can start identifying victims and coming up with possible motives."

"What's your main worry, then?"

"I'm wondering why someone would take the time to chop up twenty people into little bitty pieces. Granted, it was in the wee hours of the morning and there was a blizzard, so it would be less likely there'd be witnesses, but still."

"Why would he want the victims to remain unidentified?"

"Undoubtedly to keep us from connecting him to them, but we won't know for certain until we catch the son of a Sirulian she-dog." Leah didn't like to speculate on the details of a murder without evidence, even for Quinn. She liked to keep the early days of her investigations as non-specific as possible until the evidence started trickling in, giving her something specific she could speculate on. Right now, the only evidence she had was tiny pieces of bone and flesh and perhaps the bishop. That was way too little to build a case on or to begin speculating about who the perp or perps were.

"Are you thinking it's gang related, then? One of the big crime families dealing with traitors or some such?"

"Right now, I'm not thinking about who it could be. I doubt it was a gang or a mob since they tend to kill their victims with guns or knives one at a time, not dozens all at once."

Quinn sat silently while she digested what Leah had told her. "Anyone who could pull this off is seriously deranged and dangerous. Which means, love, that you're in danger, aren't you?"

"Yes. Which is why I've limited the investigation to myself and two other detectives." She knew Quinn worried far more than she did about her safety.

"Are they to be trusted?"

"I think so. But who knows in something like this? I'm also taking the investigation out of the precinct house."

"The fewer people who know what you're up to, the less the enemy knows."

Leah smiled. Quinn was learning. "Exactly."

There was another light knock on the door. The identifier indicated it was their waiter. Leah put her hand on her weapon, suddenly more paranoid than before talking with Quinn. She nodded at Quinn, who tapped the key that unlocked the door.

The waiter, seeing Leah had her hand on her weapon, quickly served their dinner and fled.

"Where are you taking the investigation?"

"You mean physically?"

"Yeah," Quinn said, smiling. "I know full well nothing else will be on your mind until it's over."

"I'd like to take it to your old place. It's secure. It's high-tech. It has the tools we'll need to be able to do research. There's no obvious connection to me or the team."

"Perfect choice. But if it ever comes out that you ran the investigation from the condo, the shit will hit the fan."

"It's bound to happen someday."

That was the one thing she and Quinn had been hoping they could stave off for several years. They didn't want people finding out they were together. While the prohibition against humans marrying aliens had been lifted five years earlier by the legislature, the stigma against it was still firmly in place.

Quinn was a Devarian, a fierce race who had come to Earth uninvited and refused to leave. A war had been fought and Earth had sued for peace after only six months. The humiliation of "defeat" had seeped into the human psyche. There were those who still hadn't forgiven the Devarians for winning the war, though many people in New America would never admit they'd lost to a race of aliens.

Leah had met Quinn four years earlier during an investigation of a Devarian woman murdered for being with a human man. Initially, Quinn had been looked at as a possible suspect because she'd been seen near the murder scene minutes after the victim had been killed, and because she was Devarian, but Leah had quickly cleared her. She found her intelligent, open-minded, and helpful in her investigation. The more time she'd spent with Quinn, the more she wanted to be with her. Leah had always been attracted to intelligent, tall, blond women. Everything about Quinn drew Leah to her. Quinn had asked her out, and within a few months, they had both declared their love, even though they knew Leah's career could be ended by the disclosure of their relationship. Few in the cop shop would want to work with her if she were associating with an alien. Things were changing as more and more Devarians were integrated into human society, but the changes were slow in coming.

"I can't afford to go through the department to find a safe place to work. The captain and chief like to think that all cops, except those at the Eighty-sixth, are clean. We all know it's not true. That knowledge hasn't climbed its way up the chain of command yet."

"I'd rather risk exposure of our relationship than to have you risk your life and/or career at the precinct. Is there anything I can put into the condo for you before you arrive?" Quinn asked.

"Not if you left your electronics behind."

"Yeah, they're still there. I keep hoping we'll be able to live there one day. In the meantime, Cots spends time there."

Leah hadn't yet figured out what Cots's role in Quinn's life was. Best friend? Valet? Bodyguard? So many possibilities, and when asked, Quinn was somewhat vague with her answers. Leah knew Devarians didn't like to discuss their personal relationships with humans because they were complex and not always like human families and friends, so she accepted the lack of information as part of having a relationship with a nonhuman.

They ate their dinner in silence, each lost in thought.

"I'm about to suggest something I'm sure you won't like, but I'd like you to consider it nevertheless," Quinn told her.

"Uh-oh," Leah said with a smile. She took a deep breath. "All right, tell me."

"I'd like Cots to stay with you."

"You're kidding me, right?"

Cots was also a Devarian. He was six feet seven inches tall, handsome as the day is long, charming when he wanted to be, and could pass for human with ease. Beyond his looks, though, he was trained in about 96,000 ways of killing. He'd been a soldier in a very elite division of the Devarian military before immigrating to the Americas. Quinn, like others of the ruling family on Devaria, had grown up under protection. According to Quinn, Cots had been with her since she was a child, and she trusted him implicitly. When the war ended, many of the Devarians, in a gesture of goodwill, had assumed human names. Cots had, for reasons known only to himself, chosen the name Cotsworthy. Quinn, too, had chosen a new name, since her own was unpronounceable by humans.

"What in the world would I do with him? He'd be in the way."

"No, he wouldn't, and you know it. He'd be helpful. He is discreet and wouldn't betray you or your investigation. He knows the electronics as well as I do and better than you. And it would give me some peace of mind knowing he had your back."

Leah's mind was running a mile a minute. What Quinn said made sense, but having to deal with Cots on a daily basis in the middle of a nasty investigation wasn't her idea of a good time. She and Cots hadn't much liked each other from the beginning.

Evidently, Cots thought Quinn shouldn't be involved with a human and should certainly never have married one.

When she and Quinn were finished with dinner, they sat a few minutes longer, talking about Quinn's day. During the previous four years, she'd made a fortune buying and selling real estate. She seemed to have a second sense about upcoming trends. In fact, the restaurant they were sitting in was hers, which was why they were both comfortable talking about Leah's case there. Quinn knew the extent of the security in this room. If she was comfortable with it, so was Leah.

"You leave first, love. I'll follow later. Meet you at home?" Quinn asked.

"Okay. I had planned to go back to the precinct, but there's nothing I can do there. Since my communicator hasn't buzzed since I've been here, there's nothing new."

"Good girl. Why don't we go to the condo first thing in the morning and check it out?"

"Sounds good," she said, sliding from the booth. "Thanks for dinner. It was delicious as usual."

"Did you even taste it?"

She smiled at her. She hadn't actually tasted the food. "Of course."

"Liar."

She shrugged and Quinn released the lock on the door.

"Take care out there," she said.

As she walked through the restaurant, she felt, rather than saw, eyes on her. *Am I just being paranoid? Besides, how could anyone know where I'd be?* Quinn might be right. Maybe Cots would be a nice addition to the team. Another pair of eyes might not be a bad thing.

Leah took a circuitous route home to see if she could spot who was following her. She was sure someone was but couldn't see anyone specific. There were too damned many cars on the road to get a good sighting. She wasn't so much worried about who was following her as why. None of the cases she was responsible for would make anyone want to follow her, and the murders in the field were too new for anyone to know about the details. She mentally shrugged since there was nothing she could do about it, filed away the possibility she might have been followed, and continued home to Quinn.

CHAPTER FOUR

The next morning, as Leah and Quinn were preparing to leave their apartment, she called Davidson and Fong. She told them to meet up at the food kiosk at Fifth Avenue and Sixty-third Street and call her from that location. She also told them to make sure they weren't followed.

Leah and Quinn went directly to the condo. Leah loved the space and had wanted them to live in it, but Quinn had asked whether someone might question how she could afford to live in the building, let alone on the top floor, on her cop's salary. She had been disappointed to have to agree with her, but she was right, there was no way she could afford to buy the space, so Quinn had moved into Leah's already-cramped apartment when they married. They'd talked about moving to a larger space but never seemed to have time to go looking, even with Quinn being in the real estate business.

When they entered the condo, Leah could sense there was already someone in the space. She tensed and her hand automatically went to her weapon.

"Relax, Lieutenant. Cots is here. I asked him to install some additional equipment and some additional security," Quinn said, lightly touching Leah's arm.

"I seem to be jumpy all of a sudden."

"Little wonder," Quinn murmured.

Quinn led the way behind a security screen built into a wall in the living room that, when activated, looked as if it was part of the wall. On the other side of the screen was a large room full of electronics. There were multiple screens covering each wall and the room was cooler than the rest of the condo because of all the equipment, making it so the humans working the equipment didn't sweat to death.

"Good morning, Lieutenant," Cots said with a ghost of a smile as he rose from behind one of the two desks in the room.

Leah looked at Cots closely. It wasn't like him to be so convivial around her. She had once asked Quinn if the man ever got any older or if his looks stopped changing when he hit his thirties in human years. Quinn had only laughed at her, and hadn't given an explanation. Leah hadn't seen Cots in nearly a year, and he remained unchanged. She wondered if he'd share his secret with her. Probably not. He didn't share anything about himself. Besides, it was probably a Devarian thing, which left her wondering... *Will I look my age at ninety while Quinn still looks thirty-five?* It was a disconcerting thought she put quickly from her mind.

Now, as she studied Cots, she noticed there was a decided resemblance between Cots and Quinn she hadn't really noticed before. They both had the remarkably blue eyes with the small double pupil of upper-class Devarians, Cots's hair was so dark it always reminded Leah of a bottomless lake, and both were nearly the same height. Yet another thing to wonder about—were Cots and Quinn related by more than race? Maybe they were cousins or something. She made a mental note to ask Quinn again about their relationship. She also knew that not all Devarians were related, but there was something about them that said they were more than just friends.

Leah reminded herself one of the complaints humans had when the Devarians had first arrived on their planet was that they were nearly impossible to tell apart. One of her fellow cops had remarked that "if you described one Devarian, you described them all." As time passed, it had become easier for Leah to mark individual differences.

"Good morning, Cots. Thanks for agreeing to join me."

"Anything I can do for Quinn," he said, making it clear he wasn't doing this for Leah but for Quinn.

Leah caught the look that Quinn threw Cots that all but said, "Be nice."

She smiled. According to Quinn, Cots didn't have much use for the human race. The first complaint on his list was he thought humans smelled "funny." As far as he was concerned, humans were dirty creatures who had little regard for anyone but themselves. His list of things wrong with humans was long and creative. He was able to tick them off for anyone who made the mistake of asking. With the exception of humans smelling funny, Leah had to agree with Cots's assessment of her race, but she'd never tell him that.

"I'm going to leave you two alone and go to work. Try not to kill one another while I'm away," Quinn said.

"I'll try, dear," Leah said sweetly.

Quinn shook her head and seemed reluctant to leave. Leah knew, though, she had a long day of meetings. Finally, she gave Leah a quick kiss and left.

"Cots, can I have the news on one of the screens?"

"Of course. I've finished upgrading the computers. I was finishing connecting the second desk to the system when you arrived."

Leah pulled her phone out of her pocket.

"Wait a second," Cots said as he handed her another phone. "Use this one instead. It's more secure than your police-issued phone. Your calls will be forwarded from this piece of shit," he said, indicating her police-issued phone.

Leah nodded, trying not to be offended by his analysis, and dialed Peony's number.

"Fong," she said when she answered.

"Is Davidson with you?"

"No, ma'am. We were supposed to meet here fifteen minutes ago, but she hasn't shown up yet."

Leah gave Peony the condo's address and said, "Don't give the address to anyone, including Davidson. Make sure you're not followed here. Let me know if you think you're being followed."

It's not like Davidson to be late. Her gut told her something was wrong. Leah dialed Davidson's number, but it went straight to voice mail. It wasn't like Davidson to ignore calls, either.

"News on one," Cots said.

Leah and Cots both were startled when the door chime rang.

"I'll get it. It's Fong."

"Who is he?"

"*She* is the cop working with me on a case."

"Can she be trusted?" Cots asked, voicing his belief that, with the exception of his boss's wife, there were no honest cops in the city.

"I hope so." Leah was no longer entirely sure who to trust at the moment, though she didn't want to admit it. She wasn't even sure why she was so paranoid. She couldn't remember another case that had her thinking she was being followed or made her doubt she could trust her team.

"I'll keep an eye on her."

Leah knew there was nothing she could do to prevent Cots from watching Peony, so she said nothing as she opened the front door.

"Did you hear from Davidson?"

"No. I was sure she'd be either at the office or here."

I wonder what's with Alison? I thought she was more reliable than ignoring an order. I hope she's not hurt. "Come on in."

"Is this where you live?" Peony blurted out as she looked around.

"No. It belongs to a friend of mine. I can't afford something like this on what the city pays me," Leah said, enacting the story she and Quinn had decided on.

"Why are we here?"

"We're here to try to keep the details of our case under wraps. Until we know what's going on, we need to keep a lid on this."

"I thought we knew what's going on."

"Tell me what you think we know," Leah said as she led Peony into the living room.

"We have Bishop Solomon Cohane killed in a field and then cut up. We're going to solve his murder," Peony said with more confidence than Leah felt.

"That explanation is a bit simplistic, don't you think?"

"Not as far as we're concerned. We're cops, and the only thing we should be interested in is the crime," Peony recited as if she had just been called on in a class at the police academy.

"Assuming that's true, aren't you forgetting something?"

"There were more than just the bishop in the field?" Peony asked. "I'm no expert, but from the amount of blood on that field, I'd say we're looking at dozens of victims." Peony paused. "It's true we can't ignore them, but until we find out who they were, we have no starting point to solving their murders. So we start with the bishop and see where that leads."

Cots stepped into the room behind Peony. She was startled when she finally realized there was a third person in the room with them. She whirled toward him, her hand going to her weapon.

"Relax. This is our electronics guy, Cotsworthy," Leah said. "This is Peony Fong."

Peony held out her hand to Cots. "Welcome to the team."

Cots smiled at her, took her hand in his, and said, "Thanks. Pretty name."

Peony smiled back at him, obviously charmed.

Leah's phone rang. She pulled it from her pocket and answered.

"It's Davidson, Boss. I need to talk to you in private. Can we meet?"

"Sure. Meet me at the Fifth Avenue entrance to the park," Leah said and cut the call. *This better be good. Davidson's a good cop. I hope her missing the meet with Peony is legit.*

"Give me a minute and I'll go with you," Cots said as he moved toward the door.

"Me, too," Peony chimed in.

"Neither of you are going with me. I don't want to show up with you two in tow. I want to hear what Davidson has to say. I'll be careful."

"I don't like it," Cots said.

"Me neither," Peony said, glancing at Cots.

"Duly noted."

Cots stared at her for a moment and then shrugged, clearly aware Leah wasn't going to back down. "I'll show Peony the electronics while you're out." He gave Peony a genuine smile and motioned toward the other room.

Leah nodded and only barely held back a smile. *Wouldn't it be something if the human-hating Cots fell for a human woman?*

Leah walked to the entrance of the park, which was only a few blocks away. She knew the cold would be brutal, but by the time the car was warmed up, she could already be at the park and talking to Davidson.

Davidson was at the park entrance when Leah arrived, but Leah wasn't going to stand around in the freezing cold for a short conversation, and she motioned Davidson to follow her.

"What's up?" Leah asked after they found a table at a nearby coffee shop.

"I've got to confess that I'm not comfortable being on this team," she said, unable to meet Leah's eyes.

"Why?"

"It's this case," Davidson said, making eye contact for only a second or two.

"How so?"

"I belong to Bishop Cohane's personal parish. I believe in his teachings. It would be too hard for me to be involved in investigating his murder."

That was the last thing Leah thought Davidson would come

out with. "Wouldn't it be in your best interest to help find his murderer?"

"Yes, but…" Davidson started and then paused. Leah noticed she was looking at something over her shoulder. She resisted the urge to glance behind her to see what Davidson was looking at.

Leah sighed and stopped the conversation that had nowhere to go except in circles. "It sounds like I need to reassign you due to conflict of interest; do you agree?"

"Yes. I'm sorry." Davidson looked relieved and her shoulders dropped slightly.

"Don't be sorry. I appreciate you coming to me this early. I have to wonder why you didn't say anything yesterday, though."

"I met with some people from my church last night. It wasn't until then I realized how difficult working this case would be."

"I'm going to assume you didn't give details about the case to the church people."

"No, ma'am. I only told them I might be involved in a case involving the bishop."

Leah tried not to show her irritation. Even saying there was a case involving the bishop was out of line, but it wasn't worth discussing. She'd just cut Davidson loose and be done with it. "Okay. I'll talk with the captain and let him know what's going on. In the meantime, report back to the precinct."

"Yes, ma'am. And thanks."

"No problem."

Leah was glad Davidson had come to her. She would be next to useless if her religious beliefs were so strongly held.

Leah left Davidson sitting in the coffee shop. As she exited the shop, she turned left instead of right. She was walking away from the condo, but she wanted to see if anyone was following her. Something about Davidson's request didn't sit right, and her gut told her there was something more going on. When she ducked into a doorway and looked back, no one was there.

Maybe I'm imagining things. She headed for the condo, and the feeling of being watched disappeared.

After she returned to the condo, she briefed Cots and Peony on what she found out from Davidson. "I'm going to cut her loose and tell the captain she's off our team for this case."

"That's too bad," Peony said. "I know she was really proud to be working with you."

"And she will again, hopefully. Apropos of nothing, what do you think about aliens?" With Davidson off the team, Leah was down to Cots and Peony, so she'd better know now if a potential problem was ahead.

"I don't have a problem with them. I don't know many, but the few I do know, I like. A lot. Why? Is Davidson an alien?"

What a relief. When she finds out Cots is an alien, there won't be any tension on the team.

"Not to my knowledge," Leah said.

Peony was about to ask more questions, but Cots came into the room wiping his hands. *He's probably trying to get years of dust off his hands. I guess I should have told him the janitorial staff at the precinct is less than efficient.*

"Okay, your murder board is functional once more."

"Thanks, Cots. Peony, you're with me." Leah caught the look Peony threw Cots.

Lordy, not only do I have to investigate multiple homicides, but I'm about to have to do it with a partner who has a crush on a team member, and an alien at that. Great.

She went to the murder board and pulled two comfortable chairs in front of it. After she removed the keyboard from its cradle, she turned the board on.

"Watch the news," Cots said from the doorway.

The news appeared on the screen embedded in the wall beside the murder board.

"There's been a bombing at a police station," the announcer was saying. "The reports are now coming in. Here's what we know for certain. A bomb exploded inside the Forty-fourth Precinct, destroying the building. It's too soon to know how many were killed, but our sources say it's likely there will be no survivors. No one has stepped forward to claim responsibility, and thus far, the police have no leads."

"Isn't that your precinct, Leah?" Cots asked.

She swallowed the bile rising in her throat at the thought of her friends and colleagues being killed. "Yes. I'm going down there."

"No, you're not," Cots said.

"Oh? Why not?" Leah asked, feeling her ire rise at being bossed around by Cots.

"There's a good chance this bombing might be associated with the case you're working on. Or it could be personal. Quinn said you fired some cop yesterday. Whoever bombed the precinct might have wanted to take you out. As it is, the bomber might think he has killed you. If it's not personal, the bomber will believe he's destroyed whatever evidence you already gathered, since Weston is one of only a half dozen people who know you're investigating the killing field murders, and it can't be a coincidence that the bombing occurred at this police station. The advantage is now with you since you're dead and they don't know you're looking for them."

Leah had to admit Cots had a point. If this was about the killing of the bishop and the others, and the bomber and his cohorts thought she was dead, they might get sloppy. Even a little bit careless would be helpful since she had absolutely no clues and no leads yet. If it was personal, it was most certainly Weston and they could easily nail him. But would Weston really kill all those people just to get back at Leah? She couldn't imagine even he would go that far. "All right. Peony, are you okay with that?"

"Absolutely."

"You can't tell your family you're alive."

"I don't have any family here."

"Okay." *Quinn is my only family, and she knows where I am. Thank goodness my parents and grandmother emigrated off the planet years ago.*

Leah lowered the sound on the newscast while they waited for new details. She wasn't interested in listening to a continuous loop rehashing what they'd already been told. She returned to the murder board.

Leah approached the board, which she had labeled Taconic Park Murders. She created another board she labeled Forty-fourth Bombing. She copied the photo of Weston to that board.

Cots's phone rang, and after listening to the person on the other end for a few seconds, he said, "She's okay. She's here with Peony. We've agreed we're letting the press report their deaths."

Cots held the phone out to Leah. She knew it was Quinn and took it into the electronics room for privacy.

"You're safe," Quinn said, sounding relieved.

"Yes. I'd just returned from a meet with Davidson near the park when I heard about the bombing at the Forty-fourth." Hearing Quinn's voice calmed the shocked feeling running through her and helped her focus once more.

"What was that about?"

"I'm not sure. She said she wasn't comfortable being on this investigation due to religious reasons."

"Did you believe her?"

"Not particularly, but we weren't friends or close in any way, so how am I to know whether she was telling the truth?"

"Was she at the precinct?" Quinn asked.

"I don't know. I haven't seen a casualty list yet."

"I'll send one to you."

"Thanks."

It didn't occur to her to ask Quinn how she had obtained a casualty list before the media had. She often had information ahead of any other source because she was well-connected throughout the city. Leah had learned long ago not to question how she knew things because she knew Quinn's resources were better than her own, and Quinn didn't like to discuss those resources.

"Later, love. Stay safe."

"I will. I love you," Leah said.

"And I you."

A moment later, the list of dead and presumed dead for the Forty-fourth Precinct showed up on one of the many screens in the room. She ran down the list of colleagues and friends who had been killed. Her name and Peony's were both listed under *Presumed Dead*, as was Davidson's. Weston's name wasn't on the list for obvious reasons.

Leah had previously lost friends and colleagues in the line of duty, but never so many at once. If she and her small team were right, this was one man killing dozens of people for no reason that made sense to her. These were good people a crazy person had killed. Most of them were married and had kids who would grow up without the benefit of the parent, all because of a senseless bombing. She felt tears sting the back of her eyelids as she ran down the long list of the dead. She took a couple of deep breaths to regain control. Crying wouldn't help solve the crimes on her plate or help her find whoever had killed her friends and police family.

When she returned to the living room, she was once again in control, but just barely.

"The casualty list is up on a screen in the other room if you want to take a look," Leah told Peony.

Peony looked as if she was reluctant to find out which of her friends and colleagues had died in the bombing. She got up and walked slowly into the other room. When she came back into the living room, it was clear she was holding back tears.

"You lost friends?" Cots asked.

Peony nodded. She looked like she was only barely holding it together. Cots went to her and put his arms around her. That was all Peony needed to let loose a sea of tears.

Cots was surprising Leah. She had no idea he could be compassionate. Peony was proving how sensitive she still was if she could sob at the loss of a colleague killed in the line of duty. As a cop, Leah woke up every morning knowing this might be the day that she or others would be killed, and it had hardened her over the years. She watched as Cots held on to Peony until her tears subsided. When Peony stepped away, she said, "I'm afraid I snotted on your shirt."

"Don't worry about it. It'll wash out," he said, smiling at her.

They all heard the electronic ding of one of the screens in the other room being updated. They went in to find the casualty list had been updated. Davidson's name had been removed, and thirteen additional names were moved from the presumed dead column to the confirmed dead column.

"How many people will be on the list?" Cots asked.

"A hundred twenty-four, if everyone was present. Can you keep me and Peony on the dead list? It would give us more freedom to work if the bad guys don't know we're still working the case."

"Yeah, I can do that easily enough. They removed Davidson's name."

"I saw that. She must have reported to HQ that she was in the field."

"And yet, your name remains."

"Davidson might have thought I returned to the building."

"Didn't she know you and Peony were going to be working off-site?"

"No. I hadn't told her yet."

"We figured you'd have to move us out of the precinct," Peony said. "I bet she's assuming you hadn't found a place yet. Do you want me to contact her?"

"No. Let that dog continue to sleep. I want to see where all this ends up. I sure hope someone is looking hard at Weston for this bombing."

"Why?" Cots leaned against the doorframe, looking curious and calm.

"He'd be my first suspect in the bombing if it was mine to investigate, because he hated being transferred out of the Forty-fourth, and he hated me for doing it."

"Isn't it yours to investigate?"

"Yes and no. Yes, because it may be related to the slaughter in the field somehow. But it may not be. It may be that Weston went off the deep end when I reassigned him to the Eighty-sixth," Leah said. "We need to stay focused on the killing field murders, and if we find evidence that the bombing is somehow associated with our case, then we can investigate it. Until then, the bombing belongs to the cops assigned to investigate it." She smiled. "But that doesn't mean I'm not going to keep my eyes on the bombing as well."

"I know humans can be violent for no reason, but I can't believe anyone would kill over a hundred people they knew and worked with to get even over an assignment they didn't like," Cots said.

"You don't know Weston. If you did, you'd believe it in a nanosecond," Peony said.

Leah agreed with her, but she'd been a cop too long to be surprised at any murderer's motive for killing. "Cots, run a search for Weston. Let's see if we can locate him. Also, run a search on Bishop Cohane and see if you can find anything below the surface we haven't come across yet. Can you teach Peony how to run Weston's numbers? Maybe we can find him via his devices."

Cots nodded and led Peony back into the electronics room.

Leah returned to the living room and sat staring at the murder board. It wasn't giving her anything but more questions to answer. Her mind rushed from thought to thought about the case. She examined each one and either rejected it or made a note of it. She finally gave up trying to make something out of nothing. She'd have to have patience to solve this case. Without wanting to, she let her mind wander to the bombing of the Forty-fourth. Some of the dead cops had been her friends for twenty years. She'd been invited to their weddings, raised a glass over the births of their children, and grieved with them over the loss of mutual friends in the line of duty. Now she was the only survivor of that group of friends. Who was she going to go drinking with to talk about the good old bad times?

Fifteen minutes later, Cots came out of the electronics room.

Leah quickly wiped the tears from her eyes, not wanting Cots or Peony to see her grieving for her friends.

"Leah, I'm very sorry for your loss. I can't know what it's like to lose that many friends and colleagues all at once. If you need some time alone, this can wait. But I've got something for you."

"What is it?"

"I took the liberty of running Weston's financials on a deep search—"

Leah forced herself to focus. She wanted to approach things methodically. "Hang on a second. Try to access the ME's account and see what he added to his report. I want to know if all the evidence was destroyed. It should be on the main cop server."

Leah glanced at Peony, who was standing in the doorway, and saw her eyebrows had shot up practically to her hairline, probably shocked anyone could access confidential and secret police files. Leah didn't tell her any eighth grader with a scintilla of computing skills could do it.

Cots nodded. He was smiling. He must have seen Peony's reaction, too. As the investigation progressed, Leah knew Peony's eyebrows were going to get a good workout.

CHAPTER FIVE

"The ME reports that all the killing field evidence at the Forty-fourth was either destroyed or compromised."

"What'd you find on Weston?"

"He's been receiving payments from the same offshore account for nearly six years, but he's made a hell of a lot more money than Davidson. As of Monday, he'd received payments of $720,000 over those six years. Two hours ago, his account was $250,000 richer."

"Someone paid him to bomb the Forty-fourth." *And I'll make sure he pays for that!*

"Looks like it."

Leah thought about the ramifications and variety of options in front of her. "Cots, make an anonymous call to the commissioner's office. Leave a message for her saying Weston's responsible for the bombing of the Forty-fourth. Tell her to look at his financials for circumstantial evidence, and see if you can email them to her in an encrypted file of some kind, so we can make certain she gets the information we want her to have without them finding out we're the ones sending it to her. Have you located him?"

"Not yet."

Cots returned to the electronics room when he heard the ding of one of his computers. He was back a few seconds later.

"Weston just purchased a ticket on this afternoon's off-planet shuttle to Panai."

"Make sure the commissioner has those details, too. The very least we can do is keep him here while the investigation is ongoing."

"Why would Weston kill cops?" Peony asked.

"The reasons are legion. He could be getting even for past grievances. The people who deposited the money into his account may have wanted to destroy evidence and disrupt the investigation into the murders in the field. For all we know, he may have destroyed the Forty-fourth just for fun. There are a ton of reasons he could have done it. And hell, we're not even sure he was the one who did. We're assuming."

"He's one sicko cop," Peony said with conviction.

"That's putting it mildly." Leah sighed and turned again to the board to focus on the case that was hers.

She studied the boards, trying to put the pieces together. *The people behind the murders in the field and the bombing must be feeling pretty good about how things are shaping up.* They had killed the cops assigned to the murder investigation. They had destroyed at least some of the evidence. *What would I do next if I were them? If I were smart, I'd stop there. If I were dumber than shit, I'd do something else. But what... Oh, my God.*

"Cots!" Leah yelled.

He rushed into the living room looking around for the danger he assumed was there since she'd yelled for him. "What?" he demanded.

"Cots, call Scotty and tell him to take all the killing field's evidence with him and get out of the lab. Peony, call the main switchboard at the MSI lab and tell them there's a bomb and to evacuate immediately."

"How is Cots going to pull that off?" Peony asked as she pulled her phone out of her pocket.

"Cots and Scotty go way back. Make the call."

She didn't tell her Scotty was an alien passing for human. Or that Scotty and Cots had been boyhood friends on their home world of Devaria. She wasn't sure Cots knew she knew about the two men's connection, and it wasn't her place to give away that information anyway.

Two hours later, the news began reporting a second bombing. This time it was at the police crime lab. The morgue was located in the same building. The newscaster said a casualty list would be delayed by as long as a few days while officials sorted the already dead at the morgue from those working in the lab.

"Scotty's safe. He doesn't know where to go, though, and he's scared."

Leah didn't miss the relief in Cots's expression, and she too was glad Scotty was safe. "Go get him. Contact Quinn and see if she's got a safe house available. Put Scotty there, if she does. Leave the evidence with him."

"Thanks for not leaving him in the wind. And for figuring out where they'd hit next. Damn good call." Cots gave her a nod before going to see to Scotty.

"Who's Quinn?" Peony asked. "Wait," she said as she looked around the condo, "that's not *the* Quinn, is it? The real estate mogul who's worth billions?"

Leah was impressed at how fast Peony put two and two together to figure out Quinn was the "real estate mogul." Hopefully, she wouldn't try to figure out anything further. "Yeah, it is."

"Wow. You know her? Cots knows her, too? That's so radical!" Peony gushed.

"Monitor the news channels," Leah told Peony, wanting to get her focused again. "I want to know the minute they post a list of the dead and missing in the crime lab to see who's on the list. Hopefully, Scotty's name will be on the list."

"On it," Peony said, mimicking Cots.

Leah sat in a chair in front of the privacy windows, seeing

nothing as she concentrated on the bits and pieces of information they already had. Occasionally, she'd make a note on a pad of paper she'd rested on the arm of her chair.

Peony returned to the living room a few minutes later.

"Boss, how did you know the lab was going to be the next target?"

"I didn't know for sure. It seemed logical, however, that if, and that's a big if, Weston and his friends were getting rid of the investigating team, they'd want to get rid of any physical evidence as well. It also potentially ties our cases together, which means I'm looking at it from every angle. I know pretty much all the cases going on in that precinct, and there wasn't anything bigger than the killing field murders." She shook her head. "We don't know anything for certain, so we need to try to get a step ahead, even if we're not completely sure it's the right step to take. I went with my gut."

"Oh. Right," Peony said, clearly taking that information in as she turned to go back to the secure room.

Leah continued to think and jot down notes, glad that Peony had asked the question. Questions helped her verbalize and sort through her thoughts. Cots was back within the hour.

"Scotty's safe," he said as he removed his coat and gloves.

"Good. Did he manage to get all the evidence out with him?"

"Only the partial hand and the reports from the DNA guys for sure. He told me a bunch of other stuff, but it went over my head."

While Leah doubted that what Scotty had told Cots had, indeed, gone over his head, she didn't need to know those details yet. When she needed to know, she'd ask Scotty.

"He's in one of Quinn's houses?" Leah asked.

"No. I put him at one of mine. It was faster and easier than going through Quinn and her people," Cots said.

Leah was surprised Cots owned multiple houses, but shouldn't have been considering his close ties to Quinn. It made sense, too, to put Scotty into one of his own homes rather than bother Quinn with the problem.

"I've got some more searches for you. I want you to run searches on these people," Leah told him as she handed him a piece of paper.

There was only one name listed. Peony Fong.

CHAPTER SIX

The next morning Leah was awakened by a nightmare where she was running from someone too shadowy to see, but someone she knew was going to kill her. Quinn rolled over and snuggled into her back and held her tight, murmuring, "It's okay, baby. I've got you. Go back to sleep." She tried to return to sleep, but it evaded her. She finally got up, took a shower to wash away the remains of the nightmare, got the coffeepot going, and returned to studying the murder board.

Leah continued running over the information they had. There wasn't much, not nearly enough. She wondered why no one had claimed responsibility for the killings in the field or for the bombings. *Does it mean those responsible don't have an agenda they're working from or toward? If they have no cause, then why the killings? Are they trying to hide something that required the very public bombing of a police precinct?*

"Weston's been found. He's dead," Peony said, coming into the living room. "Murdered."

"Where?"

"Near the space port. His throat was slit. The news is reporting it now."

"I made the call to the commissioner's office while I was looking for Scotty yesterday. She said she'd order Weston picked up ASAP. Obviously, they weren't in time," Cots said, coming in behind Peony.

"Do you know who she gave the order to go get him?" Leah asked.

"The chief," Cots said.

"I wonder if the cops sent to pick him up were on the same payroll as Weston or if they found him already dead?"

"Why do you ask that, Boss?" Peony asked.

"If he wasn't already dead, why would clean cops slit his throat? Wouldn't they want to bring him in and go to trial to prove he's a rogue cop and not every cop on the force is dirty? Plus, Weston probably knew too much about other dirty cops. One of the higher-ups was bound to get rid of him when he went rogue. I'm not naïve enough to think there aren't dirty cops at the top of the ladder. And if the chief chose the cops picking Weston up, I wonder if he knew they were dirty? God, I hope not. I hope the chief is clean."

"The cops sent to pick him up will say they found him dead. It will be hard to prove otherwise, won't it?" Cots asked from the doorway. "Here's the report you asked for earlier."

"Thanks," Leah said, taking the blank folder from Cots. He motioned to Peony and they left the room as Leah quickly scanned the report on Peony. Her attention was taken from the information on Peony by the newscaster on the vidscreen.

A reporter's voice intoned almost robotically as the camera panned over the still-smoking debris of the former police station. "Yesterday's bombing of the Forty-fourth Precinct was an old-fashioned bombing," the reporter said. "It was caused by a van filled with explosives being detonated near the entrance at the side of the building, which is used almost exclusively by the police. The blast leveled the building and left a crater nearly twenty feet deep."

"I'd say that was overkill, wouldn't you?" Cots asked.

"Drude, Cots! Don't sneak up on me like that! You're lucky I don't have my weapon. You're going to get yourself killed one of these days doing that." She'd learned a valuable lesson on the subject when she was a rookie cop. She'd run past an armed robber she'd been chasing, and he came up behind her and had a knife at her throat before she even sensed he was there. Luckily, her partner had finally caught up to her and grabbed the perp's knife hand and had him on the ground in a flash. Since then, she always paid attention to who was behind or around her.

"Sorry, Boss," Cots said.

"Do you think Peony knows I'm married to Quinn?"

"She may not know you're married, but she's sure you're sleeping together."

"Okay."

"Don't worry about it, Boss. She's cool."

"Good. By the way, we need to let the cops assigned to the case follow the clues we've given to the commissioner. We need to focus, and stay focused, on the murders in the field," Leah said. "If we really do find a link between our case and the bombings, and I think we will, then we'll start following that angle more closely."

Leah returned to staring at her murder boards. She wasn't seeing them because nothing had changed. Rather, she was wondering how she was going to connect the bombing of the Forty-fourth and the killing field. She thought they were connected, but she couldn't see the thread linking them yet.

When Quinn arrived home at eight, she was carrying enough takeout food to feed a small army. "I figured you guys would be hungry."

When they were all settled around the coffee table in the living room, with the dozen or so takeout containers strewn around the table, Quinn asked, "What's new?"

They explained what they knew and then told her what they didn't know.

"It sounds like you actually know less than what you don't know. Am I right?"

"You are," Leah said. "But it's early days yet."

Quinn laughed. "If I had a dollar for every time you've said that to me in the early days of an investigation, I'd be filthy rich."

"You already are," Cots murmured.

By the time they'd eaten their fill and cleaned the detritus from the living room, Leah just wanted to spend some quiet time with Quinn. "Let's all get a good night's sleep," she said.

They said their good nights and went to their separate rooms. Leah was exhausted, and as much as she wanted to snuggle with Quinn, she was asleep as soon as her head hit the pillow. She woke up later long enough to enjoy the feel of Quinn snuggled against her back and her arm thrown across her to pull her tight.

"I love you," Quinn whispered.

"I love you," Leah said sleepily.

CHAPTER SEVEN

When Leah awoke the next morning, she was alone. Seconds later, Quinn padded softly into the room with a coffee mug in each hand. She wore only a huge T-shirt. She set a mug down on Leah's nightstand and took the other to her own side of the bed.

"Good morning, love," Quinn said softly as she slid back into bed.

"Good morning. What time is it? And why are you up?"

"I heard someone in the kitchen, so I went to check. I found Cots and Peony. They looked very guilty," she said with a smile.

"What ever happened to dating and courtship?" Leah asked as she moved closer to Quinn.

Quinn pulled Leah even closer. "You've got to admit it'd be pretty hard to date and court within the confines of this condo. Sometimes things happen fast. No harm in that."

"True."

"I need to go to the office today," Quinn said, changing the subject. "I'm finalizing the purchase of several pieces of property here in the city."

"Be careful out there, okay? Check in with Cots or me a few times."

"Of course. Do you want to shower first or shall I?"

"You shower. I'm going to sit here and enjoy my coffee. Thanks for bringing it in."

Quinn kissed her lightly on the lips before getting up and heading into the bathroom. *I wish we had more time this morning.* Leah watched Quinn walk across the room taking off her T-shirt as she went. Leah wondered if she could follow her into the shower. *No. Once Quinn is up and preparing to go to work, her focus is at her office.* She heard her singing something she didn't recognize. She didn't have a particularly good voice but sang with gusto nevertheless. Leah was pretty sure Quinn didn't think anyone could hear her. She didn't so much as hum outside the shower.

When Quinn walked out of the bathroom with only a towel around her waist, Leah had a visceral reaction. She very nearly leapt out of bed and followed Quinn into her closet. She refrained only because she'd told her about her early morning meeting. When she emerged from the closet, Leah thought Quinn was as sexy dressed as she was nude. She looked away, forcing her libido into submission. She slid out of bed and went into the still-steamy bathroom. She could feel Quinn's eyes on her as she walked across the bedroom. It was truly a shame they didn't have more time this morning.

As soon as Quinn was dressed, she said, "I'm headed for the office. I'll see you later. Have a good day, love."

"You, too," Leah said as she headed for the shower.

When Leah entered the kitchen twenty minutes later, Cots and Peony were there. They were talking quietly and had mugs of coffee in front of them.

"Pancakes?" Cots asked. Leah and Peony nodded their agreement and Cots set to work. Peony headed into the living room. Leah heard the news come on.

"Anything of interest pop on Bishop Cohane?"

"He's squeaky clean and appears to be legit."

Leah wasn't sure whether she was relieved or disappointed. Maybe a little of both if she was honest with herself, and she always tried to be. "Keep digging on him."

Cots served up pancakes and sausage links. He'd cooked the sausage while he and Leah had been talking.

"Are these real?" Peony asked. "I haven't had real sausage since I left home. I'm honestly salivating."

Peony cut a sausage in half and put it into her mouth. She closed her eyes as she chewed and made what sounded suspiciously like purring sounds. "I'm in heaven. Where did you get these?"

"I don't give away all my secrets."

"Okay, then you'll have to marry me. And cook me breakfast every morning for the rest of my life." When she realized what she'd said, Peony blushed from head to foot. "Uh, what I meant was—"

"That's okay. I understand." Cots saved her from herself, and his grin made it clear he was enjoying her blunder.

"I have to admit these are wonderful. I can't remember the last time I ate the real thing, either eggs or sausages. Those soy things they try to pass off as sausages are awful," Leah said.

"These are divine," Peony said as she popped the other half of her first sausage into her mouth.

They all cleaned their plates. Peony looked like she wanted to lick the sausage molecules off hers, and only barely refrained from doing it. After putting their dishes in the cleaner, they adjourned to the living room.

Peony turned up the sound on the news. Cots only stayed a second before slipping into the secure room to resume his searches. The reporter was retelling yesterday's news, which meant the police either weren't releasing details or they really didn't have anything new about the bombings. Perhaps the police were so disorganized that no one was investigating. Leah hoped it wasn't the latter. She turned her attention to staring out the windows. She focused her attention on the killing fields, hoping she'd find something she'd missed since the last time she looked at the murder board.

"Boss, listen to this," Peony said as she turned the volume up some more.

"This just in. The governor has declared the city to be under martial law, stating his belief that the city's law enforcement is under attack. He cited the killing of hundreds of police officers and said that until they know who is responsible for the bombing of the Forty-fourth Precinct and the crime lab complex, he is taking no chances with the safety of the citizens of New America City."

Leah called Quinn. "Did you send the governor an anonymous tip?"

"No. I didn't need to. I called Robert and told him what we knew."

Leah tried to hold her temper in check. She didn't recall making Quinn a member of her team. At the very least, Quinn should have checked with her before giving their speculations to the governor. *What else has she told him?* Leah didn't bother to ask how Quinn came to be on a first-name basis with the governor, figuring she'd probably sold him a piece of property or contributed to his election.

"I need to go, babe. Let me know if I can be of any more help," Quinn said with a smile in her voice.

"Count on it. Love you," Leah said, but Quinn had already hung up.

Leah continued to stand in front of the window after she finished her call to Quinn. She had to decide how to handle Quinn jumping the gun without asking her first. She knew she was just trying to help, but that wasn't how Leah liked things done. She continued watching the traffic below without really seeing it. The privacy glass allowed her to see out but didn't allow anyone to see in. It had begun snowing again, and the flakes were, at first, large and fluffy. As the storm moved into the city, the snow began falling faster and the flakes shrank, alerting the populace many more inches would be added to the already menacing hills of snow.

Leah caught her reflection in the window and wondered when her last haircut had been. Her hair was shaggy and looked like she'd cut it herself with kitchen shears, and dull ones at that. When this case was solved, she promised herself she'd get a haircut. She brought her thinking back to the present. She felt rather than heard Cots enter the room.

"How's Peony doing?" Leah asked, turning to him.

Cots grinned, his face lighting up. "She's good. She's got a real knack for my work."

"Maybe you should start your own research company. You could hire her."

"Who would hire *me*?"

"I have no idea. But give it some thought. Change seems to be going around at the moment."

He looked at her contemplatively. "I will."

The day sped by, but they still had made no advance toward solving the murders in the park by that evening. She was frustrated because there was no movement on the case. She tried telling herself that if they had been at the precinct, they wouldn't be any further along in solving the case than they were. If they didn't catch a break soon, she might have to consider leaving the off-site workspace and going to another station so she'd have more people to work the ground. But if she was right about the bombings, she could be putting more cops in danger, and there was no way in hell she'd do that. She had to find a way to get answers without showing her hand to the outside world. *Sure. No problem.*

At eleven, Quinn still wasn't home, so Leah went to bed without her. It wasn't unusual that Quinn would work late. What was unusual was that she hadn't called to tell Leah she'd be late. *What's that about? I'm beginning to feel like my life is turning upside down and I've got no way to control it.* It wasn't that long ago that it was unheard of for people to attack law enforcement officers en masse. Yet, already the bombing had fallen off the newscasts. Had the world grown so callous? Or did they simply not have anything more to report?

She sighed and pulled the covers over herself. *Tomorrow.* Everything would still be there to deal with tomorrow.

CHAPTER EIGHT

Quinn had arrived home at two in the morning. Leah dozed on and off, but then got up four hours later. She showered and put on a turtleneck sweater, heavy sweats, and socks. She was standing in front of the windows watching it snow when Cots came in and handed her a mug of coffee. The two of them stood in companionable silence enjoying the first coffee of the day.

Peony came into the living room in a rush.

"Look at what I found," she exclaimed, pointing to the murder board.

Cots and Leah turned toward the murder board. *Please let it be good news. Or at least not awful news.* Leah and Cots stood in front of the boards and read the information Peony had uploaded. It was only a couple of sentences long, but it said the police were looking at a rogue cop by the name of Weston for the bombing of the Forty-fourth Precinct.

"Where is this from?" Leah asked.

"I found it on some guy's blog."

"Who is the guy?"

"He wouldn't use his real name," Peony explained. "He calls his blog 'The Baker Street Logbook.' What does that even mean?" Peony asked.

"It doesn't matter what it means," Leah said, not wanting to go down another rabbit hole of speculation and distraction. "He's probably just one of those news hunters. But it's good to know they're on top of things. Interesting he doesn't mention that Weston is dead. They must be keeping that quiet." She rubbed her eyes. "More questions."

"I'm hungry," Cots said. "Anybody want to join me?"

"Yeah," Peony said. "Especially if you've got more sausages."

Leah smiled. *The kid can put away food, that's for sure.* She wondered how Peony stayed as slim as she was but remembered when she was in her twenties, she, too, could eat anything she wanted and not gain an ounce. Now that she was in her forties, that was no longer true. Leah missed the good old days. *Before fields full of body parts and bombings of precincts.*

Cots was cooking when Quinn walked into the kitchen and asked, "Is that breakfast I smell?"

Leah saw she had on what they called her civilian clothes. She now wore a pair of slacks and a heavy turtleneck sweater with loafers. Leah wondered what was going on.

"It is. Turns out Cots is quite the chef," Leah said. "You're dressed pretty casually for the office this morning."

"I checked in with Klara, and all my meetings are canceled because of the storm last night. I thought I'd work from home, if that's all right with you?" Klara was Quinn's assistant and right-hand woman.

Leah wasn't sure how to answer. Obviously, it was fine that Quinn work from home. But after she'd given the information to the governor without talking to Leah first, she wasn't sure how much of the case she wanted to discuss in front of Quinn. If Quinn didn't have information, she wouldn't have any to impart to anyone, and they wouldn't have to deal with the issue of boundaries. It would be easier.

"It's all right with me," Peony mumbled under her breath when Leah didn't answer.

"I've got to go out for groceries this morning. Does anyone need anything?" Cots said quickly to change the subject.

After breakfast, Leah and Quinn cleaned the kitchen of the

breakfast debris, but neither tried to engage the other. *How can I have nothing to say to the woman I've loved for years? The problem is that I don't know where to begin.* Leah relied heavily on her gut when investigating murders, and right then her gut was telling her that Quinn's telling the governor things she hadn't told her to might not be the first time Quinn had done something like that. She wanted to know if she was right, but not enough to ask her right then.

When her phone rang, Quinn stepped out of the kitchen to take the call and Leah moved into the living room. Quinn joined Leah in the living room only a minute or two later, and they watched Cots as he stepped into his galoshes. The shoe had made a comeback a few winters earlier when the planet started to stay more wet than dry due to the perpetual winter. After shrugging on his heavy coat, he made sure it was zipped up to his chin. He added a hat made out of some kind of animal skin that had flaps covering his ears. He wound a long scarf around the lower part of his face to complete his ensemble.

"What?" he demanded when he noticed the others looking at him.

"That's quite the sartorial statement," Quinn said.

"It's thirty-five below zero out there. You can get frostbitten in less than thirty seconds in that kind of cold. Sartorial splendor is less important than having a nose." His voice was muffled, but his indignant tone came through loud and clear. He left, looking like a fully clothed snowman.

Now that they were alone, Leah decided to broach the subject of boundaries. "Quinn, what in the world made you think it would be okay with me to call the governor and give him information you heard here?"

"I guess I didn't think it would be a problem."

Leah could feel her temper rising. *How could it not be a problem for Quinn to give the governor what she knew was only speculation on the team's part?* She took a deep breath to calm her temper.

"In the future, I'd appreciate you not arbitrarily deciding to tell outsiders things about the investigation without checking with me first."

The look Quinn gave her told Leah she was having a hard time holding her temper in check, too.

"I need to go in to work after all. The phone call earlier was from the office. One of my deals is getting wobbly. I need to shore it up."

Leah didn't try to convince her to stay, and when she left without a kiss good-bye, Leah didn't protest. She needed some space to clear her head and focus on the case instead of her personal life, which needed to take a backseat right now. She busied herself by writing down all the questions she could think of, which didn't make her feel better in the least.

When Cots returned with several bags of groceries, Leah followed him into the kitchen to help him put them away. When they were finished, Cots said, "Can we go into another room? I need to tell you something and I don't want you to kill this messenger. Plus, you *cannot* confront Quinn with what I'm about to tell you. Agreed?"

Leah wasn't sure she wanted to hear what Cots was about to tell her, but if it would help end the tensions between her and Quinn, she was all ears. "Agreed," she said, leading the way to the bedroom.

Cots leaned against the wall by the window and took a deep breath before starting. "Before Quinn met you, she was dating a woman named Stephanie Grandini. By the time she'd met you, they had ended their relationship because Stephanie's father didn't like aliens." Cots paused.

The name Grandini sounded familiar, but she couldn't put her finger on why. She shrugged to let Cots know she didn't know who he was talking about.

"Stephanie is the daughter of Stephan Grandini. He was the mob boss who was gunned down in front of a restaurant in midtown where he'd gone to have lunch with his daughter."

The light bulb went on. Leah remembered the case. Another precinct had caught the murder, but she remembered being surprised when it turned out to be a disgruntled employee who thought he'd be chosen to head the family; instead of running the family, he'd ended up on a penal planet serving a life sentence. As she recalled, he'd been shanked a few years later and died.

Cots took a deep breath and looked directly at her. "Stephanie took her father's place as head of the family. And two years ago, Quinn started seeing her again for the occasional meal, etc."

"Are you saying Quinn's been cheating on me with Stephanie Grandini for two years?" Leah's stomach churned and she felt clammy.

Cots, looking miserable, said, "Yes."

"Why are you telling me this?"

"Because I think Quinn is a shit, and as much as I didn't want her to marry a human, I think you're better than she deserves. And I think she may be sharing stuff she hears here with Stephanie. I've heard her talking on the phone, and from her voice I'm pretty sure that's who she was talking to. She was telling Steph about that case you had where the politician was killed by his wife. I have no idea why she would give Stephanie information you'd shared with her. I've tried, but I couldn't plug up the holes in the security surrounding this case since we openly talk in front of her."

"Cots, how do you know she's cheating?" Leah asked in a whisper.

"She wasn't discreet about having dinner with Stephanie on a regular basis. When I asked her about it, she changed the subject. Quinn became secretive, so I tapped her phone. It was crystal clear what they were up to."

Leah's mind began reeling. *How could she? How could I not know about the affair? How could I not know about her sharing information with Grandini?*

Leah knew Quinn was sharing information with the governor, too. Not knowing what else to say, she said, "Leave me alone, okay? I need to process this and its implications."

As Cots got to the door, Leah said, "Cots? Thanks for telling me. I can only imagine what it took for you to decide to do that."

"You're welcome. Like I said, Quinn is a shit and has been since she was little." Cots turned and left the room, quietly closing the door behind him.

Leah was stunned. She sat on the edge of the bed trying to get her head around what Cots had told her. One by one, puzzle pieces began clicking into place; she remembered a half dozen cases where information had been leaked, but she couldn't ever figure out who on her squad could be leaking that information. It made sense now that it had been Quinn. To say nothing of the incoming phone calls that she'd leave the room to have, and the many times Quinn worked, or said she was working, until midnight or two o'clock.

She didn't think she'd ever have a complete picture of Quinn's perfidy. She was sure, however, that her career as a cop was over. She knew she would resign in light of what she knew of Quinn's betrayal. Even if no one else knew, Leah knew her wife was involved with the head of a mob family.

As much as Leah wanted to focus on the killing field murders, her mind kept returning to Quinn. *Who is this woman? God knows she's not stupid, so did she really not figure out that if it became known she consorted with criminals, I would be guilty by association? Or did she really just not give a rat's ass how it would affect me? Who is Stephanie Grandini? Why did I not know about her? I know of Stephan, her father, but not that his daughter took over as Godfather. I must have been absorbed in a case at the time. What is the relationship between her and Quinn? I'm sure when we got together Quinn and I both talked about our exes. I'm also sure the name Stephanie Grandini would have raised a flag—a big, bright red flag.* The questions went round and round, and the frustration built until she thought she'd explode.

At nine, there was a tap on her bedroom door. She opened it and found Cots with a tray. "You need to eat something. You haven't eaten anything since breakfast."

"I'm not hungry, but thanks for thinking of me."

"It doesn't matter whether you're hungry or not," Cots said. "You need to feed your body."

"You sound like my mother," Leah said with a smile. "Leave the tray. I'll eat it after I shower."

"Nice try. If it's all the same to you, I'll stay until the food is gone," Cots said.

"Oh, for God's sake. Come in, then."

Cots set the tray on the foot of the bed. Leah uncovered a couple of the dishes, and the aroma emanating from them made her stomach growl. She ate a few bites from each one, hoping that would satisfy him and he'd go away. It didn't and he didn't leave.

As she sipped the wine he'd brought in, she asked the question she needed to have an answer for and, at the same time, dreaded knowing the answer. "Why did you really tell me about Quinn?"

"I watched you when you found out Quinn had told the governor what we were using as a working hypothesis. I don't think any of it was making sense to you. I think all that is a distraction, as is Quinn's betrayal."

"A distraction?" Leah asked. *Surely he can't think Quinn's cheating on me is a "distraction."*

"You don't know Quinn like I do. I grew up with her. She's only interested in this case as a means of gaining information that she can pass on to the people who might find it interesting. I'm pretty sure she hasn't given a thought to how all this, plus the affair with Stephanie, will affect you. I know you love her and trust her, and I think both are misplaced."

"I don't know whether to thank you for having my back and telling me or take my weapon out of my drawer over there and shoot you," Leah said. She could see the relief in Cots's eyes that she was able to joke about it.

Cots said, "I'll be in the secure room if you need me." He picked up the tray and left the room.

Leah decided she couldn't think about Quinn anymore. As a cop, she knew better than to jump to conclusions about a "suspect." As Quinn's wife, though, she didn't want to believe a word Cots had told her. Without a confession from Quinn's own mouth, she'd reserve her judgment. She knew that didn't resolve any issue, but it was easier than having to deal with the roller coaster her emotions were on.

Quinn hadn't come home the night before. She'd called and said she was still working and it was easier to stay at her office. She'd done that a time or two before, and normally, Leah didn't think anything of it. But last night, it grew like a cancer until Leah had been sure Quinn was with Grandini. She admitted to herself she was glad Quinn hadn't come home because she didn't want to have to talk about what was going on between them or why Quinn had lied by omission about Grandini. Leah mentally shook her head, trying to clear it of thoughts of Quinn and Grandini. She was tired of thinking of them. She needed to get her head back in the game and focus on the murders in the park. Leah took her coffee mug into the electronics room and sat at the empty desk in the back.

Leah was beginning to think the killing field murders would go unsolved. With the police department in total disarray, she was probably the only one still working an active case that wasn't directly connected to the bombings. Her DNA evidence could be said to be compromised in Scotty's evacuation of the crime lab, and the physical evidence he'd gathered from the killing field had been destroyed in the bombing. All Scotty had with him were the partial thumb with the bishop's DNA and hardly anything more. She had nothing. Unless she got a confession, her case was going nowhere. First, though, she had to have a suspect to question and hope that a confession would follow. She sighed and rested her head on the desk. "I hate being stuck."

"What would you normally do?" Peony asked.

"I'd go back to the crime scene to see what I might have missed when I was there when the body was discovered."

"Would it be helpful to return to the killing field?"

"It's under at least four feet of snow. It wouldn't surprise me if the snowplows have started using the field as a dumping ground. By the time the snow melts, the field will have been thoroughly compromised."

"What would be the best-case scenario here, Boss?"

"A valid suspect would be nice. Right now, we don't have a single one."

"What about Grandini? Cots said she's a mobster who knows Quinn, and Quinn has been telling her what's been going on. Is there anything there?"

Great. Cots told Peony about Grandini's involvement with Quinn. I should be angry with him for telling both of us, but I can't be. Not really. Why not? I should be ready to go ballistic, and yet, here I am being relatively sensible. "I'm hoping she becomes a suspect. But for all the theories we've got, we don't have a single element of proof against her."

"So we need something that links Grandini to the bishop, then. Right?" Peony asked. "What kind of something?"

"Something that proves there's a connection, that Grandini knew the bishop. We'll recognize it when we see it." Leah liked that Peony was asking the right questions. It pulled her out of her circular thinking and kept her in the game. She motioned Peony to follow her to the murder board.

They sat in silence studying a murder board that had hardly changed since the first day they were in the condo. They'd made no progress. They weren't even a tiny step closer to resolving the murders.

"Ask Cots to put everything he has on the bishop onto the murder board."

Peony went into the security room. Within a minute, articles and photographs began popping onto the board. A full mug of coffee appeared on the table beside her.

"Thanks," Leah said without looking away from the murder board.

"You're welcome," Quinn said softly.

She didn't, couldn't, look at her. "What are you doing home?" she asked.

"I took care of business and cleared my schedule for the afternoon. It's much more interesting here than at my office. And since I'm in 'mourning' for you, no one will think it's unusual that I left the office early."

"This isn't just early. This is obscenely early for you."

"Still, no one will comment. What are you doing?"

Leah was unsure whether to share anything with Quinn, but she didn't want to not share with her either. After all, she had no proof of Quinn's perfidy. She only had Cots's word and supposition, but she would find out at some point. Right now, she needed to set aside her personal life and solve the multiple murders in the killing field.

"Trying to find anything that will move the killing field investigation forward."

"What does the evidence tell you?"

"There *isn't* any physical evidence. We're pretty sure it was destroyed in the bombing. The only thing we know with some certainty is that one of the bodies in the field belonged to Bishop Solomon Cohane. Other than that, there are no definite connections to anyone."

"That's pretty slim evidence to solve a lot of murders."

"Slim is putting it mildly. It's more like nonexistent."

"What's your gut telling you?"

My gut is screaming you're a cheating bitch. But her heart was trying hard to disagree, and she shook the thought away. "Nothing right now. I need to find one solid lead on who the people in the field are. Then I need a connection between that person and the bishop."

"Why?"

"Because I also need to know whether the bishop was the target, thus making the others in the field collateral damage, or vice versa."

"We don't know enough about the bishop other than his occupation to even speculate on why he was killed," Peony said.

"Good analysis," Leah said. "Cots, you did the search on the bishop. Any hints in anything you found?"

"None. His personal life is shrouded in secrecy," Cots said. "His public persona, however, is full of good deeds done by a good man."

"Then how are we ever going to solve these murders?" Peony asked.

"The way we always solve crimes, and the way we should have been working this all along. We'll sift through the evidence Scotty gives us. We'll gather information from every source we can find. Somewhere in that evidence and information, answers will begin to emerge. It will be tedious and we'll be tempted to skip steps and jump to conclusions. But we won't. We'll carefully build our case and get whoever killed all those people," Leah said.

Leah knew she sounded more optimistic than she felt. Stuck in the condo until the case was solved wasn't her idea of the best way to conduct an investigation. In reality, being out in the field wouldn't help resolve this case, not to mention that she was still listed as missing and presumed dead. Cots would have to be her legs for the time being. She also knew she'd have to back off wanting Grandini to somehow be involved in this case, as there wasn't a shred of evidence to point them in her direction. Leah knew she'd let her own feelings get into the middle of this investigation, and she knew she couldn't continue to let them cloud the facts. She needed to rectify that right now.

"Where do we start?" Peony asked, looking like the young, eager cop she was.

"We'll start with the bishop. Cots, have you got everything you can find on him?" Leah asked.

"Yes. I've got a bot out in the ether waiting for his name to appear somewhere. It'll grab the information and send it back to us if anything pops up. But we're current as of last night."

"You and Peony compile the information. Distill it into something useful. When you've done that, we'll go over what you've got and go from there."

"On it, Boss," Peony said, sounding much like Cots.

Cots frowned as he followed Peony into the secure room.

Leah asked Quinn, "Don't you need to go back to work?"

"Yeah, but this is so much more interesting."

"More interesting than buying and selling property at all hours of the night and day? That's new." Leah couldn't keep the sharp tone from her voice.

"I think I'm having a midlife crisis," Quinn confessed.

"I thought you told me that Devarians lived to be in their hundreds. How can you be having a midlife crisis now?"

"They do, but I'm an early flower. Is that the correct saying?"

Leah smiled. It wasn't often that Quinn was unsure of herself. Seeing Quinn even a little vulnerable tugged at Leah's heartstrings. "You meant to say 'bloomer,' but I understood what you meant. Maybe you're bored and only need to come across a nice, juicy piece of property to get back into the swing of things."

"Maybe I'll retire," she said more to herself than to Leah. "We could travel."

"Hey, buddy, I've got a job and I can't retire for another twenty years or so." *At least, I have a job for now. If it's ever revealed my wife knew and consorted with the mob, my job will be over anyway.* Her worry about the future grew like a tsunami. But what if that was part of the answer to fix their relationship? Would Quinn walk away from Grandini so they could start over somewhere else? *Does that mean she's not cheating on me after all? Maybe Grandini is just an ex who is still a friend. And maybe I'm just grasping at straws.* As desperately as she wanted to believe it, instinct told her that wasn't the case.

"You don't need to work." Quinn returned to an old and touchy subject.

"Right now I need to solve the killing field murders. We'll talk about your midlife crisis later, okay?"

"Okay," she said, clearly already making travel plans. She left to retrieve her computer from her bag near the front door and then returned looking stressed. "Someone delivered something to you." Quinn's voice shook slightly.

"What is it?"

"An envelope addressed to you."

Leah could see the wheels turning in Quinn's head as it occurred to her that someone had breached her security system and delivered an envelope to her front door. They were no longer safe.

CHAPTER NINE

C ots," Quinn yelled.

"Yeah?" Cots darted into the room with Peony right behind him.

"How the hell did someone get into the building to deliver this?" Quinn demanded, waving the envelope.

"What are you talking about?" Cots asked.

"I found this slipped under the door," Quinn said.

"What is it?" Cots put his hand up to take it, but Quinn kept waving it like it was on fire.

"It's an envelope, and it was under our door."

"I can see that much," Cots said. "Let me have it before you open it. I'll run some tests. Maybe we'll catch a break and we'll find out who delivered it."

Quinn followed Peony and Cots back into the secure room, leaving Leah in the living room by herself. It was still snowing, although not as heavily. The snowplow had been by again but was obviously unable to keep up with removing the rapidly accumulating snow. Her mind drifted to what it would be like to get up in the morning in January and see flowers and trees with leaves on them. Better yet, what would it be like not to have to wear ten pounds of outerwear every day? Or spend a half hour getting ready to go out to get a package of coffee? She could almost imagine it, but not quite. Reluctantly, she brought herself back to the present.

Although it was midafternoon, the clouds and snow made it look like dusk. She couldn't make out the details of the many shadowy objects on the sidewalks. They could be people or trash cans. She was sure someone was watching the condo. She could sense them out there. Too many years of being a cop told her that it wasn't just another flight of fancy, like wondering what it would be like to see green living things in the middle of winter. She knew whoever was watching couldn't see her because of the privacy glass, but it felt creepy nevertheless. *Who found us and how?* Her gut said that it was Grandini who had found them, but how, and why? Quinn was the obvious answer. But why would she tell Grandini? Pillow talk? *Please don't let it be Quinn who told Grandini where we are.*

Before Leah could start that endless loop over again, Quinn returned to the living room and sank into a chair near Leah's.

"Cots is trying to see if there are any fingerprints on the envelope before he lets us open it."

"Quinn?"

"Hmm?"

"Was Stephanie Grandini ever in this condo?" Leah didn't want to think what it might imply if the answer was yes, but she had to know. If Cots was right, and Quinn was sharing information with Grandini for reasons other than just intimate talk, Leah needed to know. And if it was at all connected to her case, she definitely needed to know. No matter how much it hurt to know the truth.

"You're thinking she sent the envelope?" Quinn asked, obviously avoiding answering her question.

Leah didn't miss the fact that Quinn didn't pretend not to know the name. "It's a possibility, isn't it?"

"But that would mean she knows you're still alive."

"Does Grandini know this is where you lived? Was she ever here?"

"Yes," she answered without elaborating or looking at Leah.

Leah's heart sank at the answer. "Does she know you and I are married?"

"Yes, I told her a few weeks before we married that I was going to marry you."

"So she could assume this is where I'd come if I were going to conduct an investigation in secret. Or if I wanted to hide."

"How would she know you were conducting an investigation outside the precinct?"

"If she knew we were married, she could guess I'd come here, don't you think?"

"You're sounding paranoid, love," Quinn said.

"There are no fingerprints, no DNA, no chemicals, and it's not a bomb," Cots said as he entered the living room and handed the envelope to Leah.

Leah carefully opened it and removed a folded piece of paper. She slipped the envelope into the evidence bag that Peony held out for her. She slowly unfolded the piece of paper, hoping Cots was right about there being no chemical agents.

"Lieutenant Samuels, you need to look no further than your wife's lover for a suspect."

The note was unsigned, of course. They had a typed note incriminating Stephanie Grandini in the killing field murders, but nothing to substantiate the accusation, not even a partial fingerprint. What good was it except to act as a distraction and send them on a wild-goose chase? But if it was true, then someone was trying to help. Regardless, the author of the note knew way more about her personal life than she was comfortable with. And she could kiss her career good-bye if an anonymous note writer had been willing to incriminate a mob boss in a murder, because once the police began questioning Grandini, the paper would get hold of the story and her personal life would be grist for their mills. Leah looked at Quinn, but her expression was unreadable, her shoulders stiff and slightly raised.

"What can we surmise from this note?" Leah asked Peony.

"That he or she knows about your marriage to Quinn, that she knows about Quinn's extramarital affair with Grandini, and she's telling you she knows where you are. She also thinks that now that you know about Quinn, you'll try to make the accusation in the note stick to Grandini." She paused. "Or it's straight up telling us who is responsible, and there's nothing more to it than that."

"Good analysis. What should we do about it?" Leah asked.

"Take Grandini into custody and question her about any involvement in the killing field murders," Peony said.

"What, exactly, do we have that would allow us to question her?"

To Peony's credit, she sat thinking before answering. "We have nothing to tie her to the murders."

"Exactly. This is a wild-goose chase. My gut tells me it's meant to distract us from proceeding with our investigation of the murders. It's too simple, too convenient to have a suspect handed to us. So, who might do something like this?" Leah asked.

Peony didn't have an answer. Then a thought flew through Leah's mind. "What if the note isn't really about the investigation?"

"What do you mean?"

"What if the writer of the note simply wanted me to know about Quinn and Grandini?" Leah asked.

Her gut told her it was Grandini. *She wants me to know about her and Quinn. But why? And why now?*

"I think that's quite a stretch, Leah," Quinn said. "Are you going to believe an anonymous note writer or me? Why would you do that?"

Cots and Peony both left Leah and Quinn alone to have a conversation that had nothing to do with either of them or the case they were investigating.

Leah refused to give up Cots for having told her the truth. "All right, Quinn. I'll ask you straight out. Are you having an affair with Grandini, and have you been feeding her information about my cases?"

"Fuck it, Leah, how could you possibly think that?" Quinn asked before storming out of the room and slamming the bedroom door.

Leah's heart sank in a sea of disappointment. She knew, then, with certainty, the allegations against Quinn were true because Quinn only ever stormed out of a room when she was cornered. Otherwise she'd have stayed and tried to talk her way around the issue. She would no longer be able to trust Quinn, but strangely and to her immense surprise, she could continue to trust Cots.

The vid screen with the news on it dinged softly to alert them that there was breaking news about to be announced. Leah hadn't even noticed the vid screen was still on.

"Should I turn it up?" Peony asked, returning to the living room followed by Cots.

Leah nodded, glad for the distraction.

"The police are reporting that they've received reliable information about the bombing of the police station house," the reporter intoned solemnly. "Their sources indicate that a gang calling themselves the Devarian Kings have taken responsibility for the bombing. We'll have more as this important story develops."

"They're making that up," Cots said hotly.

"Who is 'they'?" Leah asked.

"The police," he said. "Someone. It's a lie."

"Cots, we're pretty sure we know who's responsible for the bombing. And with luck, the team investigating it will be able to prove it was Weston. But we have to stay undercover until we solve the murders in the killing field."

"In the meantime, the vigilantes will begin hunting down Devarians, as will the police," Cots said bitterly.

"What would you have us do? Abandon the killing field

investigation, go running out into the open to become targets?" Leah asked.

"No," he conceded, looking defeated rather than angry.

"The faster we close the investigation and figure out how everything is connected, the quicker we can arrest the murderers and exonerate the Devarians."

"What will happen if we can't solve the murders, Boss?" Peony went to Cots's side and took his hand.

"We may have a civil war on our hands. People of both races have been itching for a rematch of the Devarian War for years." Leah wondered what the point was of starting a civil war. How would the players in this game benefit? *More questions without answers.*

"Why are the Devarians wanting a rematch? They won the war," Peony said, looking up at Cots.

"They want revenge for years of feeling unwelcome," Cots said.

"For feeling unwelcome? What are they, ten?" Peony asked incredulously.

Leah laughed. "Both sides are." She wondered if this new information had any bearing on the killing field case. She decided it didn't and was only a consequence of the city's people being afraid. *The sooner we get the case solved, the sooner things will return to some semblance of normalcy.* "Cots, why don't you call the governor and drop an anonymous tip that Weston was responsible for bombing the Forty-fourth and the crime lab complex. That might cool down the urge to blame the Kings, who we know for certain are innocent."

"Why don't I call him and have a chat?" Quinn asked as she returned to the living room.

Leah had temporarily forgotten Quinn was in tight with the governor. *But who the hell doesn't she know?* "Go ahead." Leah watched as Quinn dialed a number from memory. *Everything she does convinces me she's betrayed me, but with how many people?*

"Robert, it's Quinn," Quinn said when the governor answered his phone. She was quiet as the governor spoke. "I didn't get to ask you earlier. How are Carole and the kids holding up?"

Leah rolled her eyes. She was too used to being a cop and getting right down to what she needed to know. This business of polite chitchat was way beyond her abilities. *Wait! Did she just say she'd called the governor earlier? Why?*

"Someday, Robert, someday," Quinn said.

Leah wondered what the governor had asked.

"Listen, Robert. I know for certain the Devarian Kings aren't responsible for the bombings, so why are the police saying it was them?"

Leah watched Quinn's expression, but she wasn't giving anything away.

"Yes, I'm sure. I wouldn't lie to you, you know that," Quinn said, cutting her eyes briefly toward Leah. "Besides, what proof is there that they're involved?"

Quinn listened to the governor. "That's all I'm asking, Robert. Tell your police to look at a guy named Weston from the Forty-fourth precinct. He was moved to the Eighty-sixth. I have it on good authority he's your bomber." She listened again, a small smile playing on her lips. "Yes, let's do get together for dinner. Thanks for listening."

Leah was amazed Quinn had acquired the skill to chat up people. She wasn't sure why she was surprised, considering she was in the business of buying and selling. But Devarians were known for their stoicism and, some said, their lack of being able to laugh. Leah's skills in small talk weren't exactly stellar either. She tried, but she always ended up skipping all the niceties because she wasn't really interested in the answers to the chitchat questions.

When Quinn hung up, she was silent. When she finally realized Leah was staring at her, Quinn said, "Something is going on with Robert. He was abrupt and seemed to be playing at being affable. He was holding something back, I feel certain. Maybe there was someone in the room with him. Maybe I'm getting paranoid, too."

"We should all be paranoid at this stage. We don't know who we can trust." Leah knew her words had bite to them, and when Quinn flinched slightly, she felt bad. But only fleetingly when she thought about the miles of secrets that lay between them.

"It doesn't make any sense. Let's add this to the page that's headed 'Things That Make No Sense About This Case,'" Leah said with a tired smile.

"We have a page for that?" Peony scanned the board, searching.

"Only in my head."

"Why don't you simply call Grandini and ask her if she's involved in any way?" Quinn asked.

"Do you think she'd be truthful?" Leah asked. She really didn't think Grandini was involved. But then, she was a mob boss, so who the hell knew what she was capable of? It was a lead, and as much as she hated it, she'd have to follow it.

"If she isn't involved, she'll be truthful. If she is, she won't. That would be my guess," Quinn said.

"Set up a meet with her for me." Leah wanted to see for herself what Grandini's reaction to her questions would be. And she wanted to meet the woman Quinn had betrayed her with. Leah had run out of options and was tired of hiding in the condo.

"Do you think that's wise, Boss?" Peony asked.

"No. But we've got to get this case closed sooner rather than later. Someone wants us to think Grandini is a suspect in the murders. I can hardly send around uniforms to pick her up, can I? So if I want to ask her questions about her possible involvement, I need to meet with her. I need to look her in the eye, not talk to her on the phone."

"We don't have time to secure somewhere. Nor do we have the people to keep you safe." Peony looked frantic.

"Peony, do you really think Grandini would kill me during a meet?"

"Possibly."

"Nevertheless, we're going to do this. Quinn, can you and Cots make this happen?" Quinn had admitted to knowing Grandini, but nothing more. But she hadn't balked at setting up the meeting, either. *Is she willing to put me in harm's way? Or does she think Grandini is innocent, too? Or is she trying to prove she's the innocent one by showing me she has nothing to hide about Grandini by putting her wife and her lover in the same room and hoping they don't kill one another?*

"Yes. Give us an hour."

"Good. In the meantime, I want some quiet time to review the files Cots has compiled on the bishop. I want to see if there's anything we may have missed on our first look at him."

Leah took a seat in front of the murder board and brought up the files on the bishop. Peony sat in the chair next to Leah as if the two of them had been working together for years instead of days. Leah tried to focus on the information she was reading, but her mind kept wandering. *Am I pursuing Grandini because of her relationship with Quinn? I hope not. I'm a better cop than that and know not to let personal feelings guide my investigation.* She needed to move this case forward, if only an inch. The only way to do that was to begin eliminating the chaff from the wheat.

CHAPTER TEN

An hour and a half later, Leah felt she knew the bishop well. If he was less than honest, Cots's research hadn't found it. Why then was he killed? According to Cots, he was so clean he squeaked.

But who else was in that field with him? Before Leah could begin forming answers to the two key questions to this investigation, Cots and Quinn returned to the living room.

"We've got your meeting with Grandini set. There are conditions, of course," Quinn said.

"Of course. What are they?" Leah leaned back in her chair and looked at Quinn, and felt a tidal wave of sadness sweep over her.

"You both will be accompanied by only one person. If she sees anyone who looks like a cop, she's leaving. And if we see anyone whose looks sets you off or there's more than one mobster lurking about, we'll leave."

Leah laughed. "These days, everyone I meet looks like a criminal. We might be in trouble. Where is the meet taking place?"

"She suggested out of doors in an hour." Quinn sat down beside her.

"What? It's got to be thirty degrees below zero. We'll both have frostbite before we say more than three words to one another," Leah said.

"That's essentially what I told her. I told her you were not going to expose yourself to the weather. The meet had to take place inside. So she suggested the Rigatoni Restaurante on Seventy-fifth."

"Don't the Grandinis own the place?" Cots asked.

"Yes. So I rejected it. I suggested Mama's Mexican. But she knew I owned it and rejected it."

"Where did we end up?" Leah didn't care where they weren't meeting. She wanted to get this over with.

"The Museum of Natural History. It's public and, in this cold, tourists will be scarce. Even the hardiest tourists won't venture out in this weather to go to a museum. At least, that's our thinking. It will be warm, and there are places where the two of you can talk in private."

"I hope you two know it's possible that her phones are tapped by the Feds. We need to change the location at the last possible moment," Peony said.

"She does know her phones are tapped. But she uses the same technology as Cots does to secure her personal phone," Quinn said.

"How much time do I have?" Cots asked.

"We need to leave in twenty minutes," Quinn said, glancing at the clock on the murder wall.

"Wait," Cots said. "Why are you going in with Leah? I should be going with her."

"Or me," Peony said. "After all, I am a cop."

"I'm going because I know Stephanie better than either of you. I know her body language, and I'll know if Leah's in danger. Also, I'll know when she's lying. And Stephanie said Leah's second person had to be me or there'd be no meet," Quinn said.

"Come with me, Leah," Cots said, sounding resigned and giving up the fight.

Leah and Cots went into the secure room where Cots put a tiny listening device on the back of the black turtleneck sweater she was wearing. He put it beneath the fold in the sweater at the neck, a place few people would think to look. He attached a second device to her scalp, behind her right ear. She noticed that he kept looking over her shoulder at the door, and his jaw was clenching constantly. He was far more nervous than he should be, and that made her *really* nervous.

Finally, Cots said in a voice so low that Leah had to strain to hear him, "Be careful, Leah. Stephanie hates you. She believes you took Quinn away from her. Quinn gave her my phone technology, so she'll know what to look for. Watch your back."

Baffled, Leah was about to ask for details but decided to take the warning at face value.

"Peony and I will be in the van outside the museum," Cots said. "We'll hear everything you say. If you feel you're in danger, I want you to work the word 'triangle' into your conversation. That will tell us to come get you."

Actually, she thought it was sweet, and stupid, for Cots and Peony to come rushing to her rescue. Grandini probably had an army stashed in and around the museum while Leah's army consisted of herself and three others, two of them civilians. *I'd say the odds are in Grandini's favor on this one.*

"We've got to go, Leah," Quinn said, stepping into the room.

"We're done here," Cots said, looking for all the world as though he hadn't just given her a serious warning.

Leah went into the foyer at the front door and opened a safe embedded into the wall. She took out her holster and put it on over her sweater. She took her primary weapon, ensured that it was loaded, and slipped it into the holster.

"Where's Peony?" Leah asked.

"I just sent her to start warming up the van," Cots said.

"You can't go in armed," Quinn said. "She'll expect that."

"I'm sure as hell not going in without a weapon. You can bet she'll be armed."

"If she knows you're armed, she may walk away," Quinn said.

"Then she walks. I'm not going into this situation unarmed," Leah repeated.

"At least carry this as a backup, then," Quinn said, taking something from Cots that reminded Leah of a lemon reamer.

"What the hell is this?" Leah asked.

"It's a weapon. Take it." Quinn held it out for her to take.

Leah took the device from her and immediately felt ridiculous. It was only five inches long. She wondered if one of Grandini's goons drew a gun on her if she would be expected to poke him with it.

"This is a laser gun. Powerful and dangerous. It was developed on Devaria," Quinn said.

"It's also illegal here." Leah wasn't sure where the hell to carry the kind of weapon Quinn had just told her it was.

All weapons except those issued to and carried by domestic police officers had been banned seven years earlier after centuries of efforts to do it. Of course criminals had refused to give up their weapons, but there were far fewer killings with guns by civilians since the law-abiding citizens had turned in their weapons. Luckily for all concerned, the common criminals had no way to replace their weapons and were more interested in killing each other than civilians. Usually, if a civilian was killed by a gun, it was a case of being in the wrong place at the wrong time. The weapon Quinn was giving her wasn't issued by the police department and was, therefore, illegal. She could be arrested for carrying it. Who knew what would happen if she actually had to fire the thing.

"Let's not quibble over details," Quinn said with a smile. "Let me show you how to fire this beauty."

The "beauty" was light and fit into her hand as if it had been made for her. It occurred to her to wonder if Quinn had had it made for her. There was no trigger per se. Instead, where the handle met the business end of the weapon there was what felt like a small toggle switch.

"You can't test fire the gun without putting a soccer ball–sized hole in the wall," Cots told her. "You're going to have to trust me that it's deadly."

"Okay," Leah agreed, not wanting to test Cots's assessment of the damage it could do.

"Give me your police-issued weapon. You can't wear it into this meet."

Leah took off her weapon and immediately felt vulnerable and naked. *This is truly a stupid idea.* But Quinn and Cots were right. If they found out she was wearing a weapon, they would assume she was acting in bad faith and probably kill her and Quinn before she'd have a chance to pull her lemon reamer on them.

And there's no way I'm going to pull a citrus reamer from my pocket in front of a mob boss. If she couldn't get it to fire or it didn't do what Cots and Quinn thought it would, she'd become the laughingstock of the city in a matter of hours, assuming she lived to tell the tale. Her days as a cop would end shortly thereafter not only because she had an illegal weapon, but because once the media got hold of what she'd done, every criminal in town would be laughing themselves silly every time she tried to arrest one of them. *Not that I'd live long enough for that to happen.* And what if Grandini's goons patted her down? They'd find a lemon reamer in her pocket. This was not a good idea.

"I'll meet you at the end of the corridor," Quinn said, stepping out of the condo.

She's probably calling Grandini to tell her we're on our way. Or maybe she's just nervous.

"What's the safe word?" Cots asked, testing her.

"Triangle."

"Okay, we're good to go," Cots said. "The van's ready, too."

"How do you guys have a surveillance van already?" Leah asked Quinn as they headed up the stairs to the floor above their condo.

"Cots has a few carefully chosen clients," Quinn said.

While that didn't explain the van, or anything, really, it would have to do for time being. They exited the stairwell and went down a long, well-lit corridor. At the end of the corridor, they went through a door on their right that led to a flyaway, an enclosed bridge, that crossed over the street below and into another building.

Inside the building, Cots led them to a fire door, used a pass key to open it, and they went down a flight of stairs, out into another hallway, through a door, across another flyaway, and exited into a third building two long blocks away from the condo. They went down the stairs to an underground parking structure for the building's residents. A black van was parked at the back of the structure. Cots used his remote entry code to open the van for them. Peony got out of the driver's seat and followed Leah into the back of the van while Cots went to the driver's side door and Quinn to the passenger side. They didn't have to wait long for the van to be warmed up and ready to go. Leah could only imagine what the residents' heating bills were like since they chose to heat their garage. Maybe Cots lived in this building. She'd have to ask him some day. She realized she'd come to both like and respect him over the last few days and hoped she'd have the chance to talk to him again when this was over. She replayed his warning about Grandini and forced herself to focus.

Cots took them out of the garage and onto the street. It was the first time Leah and Peony had been out of doors in what seemed like weeks but in reality was only a few days.

Cots drove them on one-way streets whenever possible. It was safer than trying to negotiate two-way streets that had become clogged with snow by the onslaught of the long series of winter storms that had hit the city. If you met a car coming toward you, it became a waiting game to see who would back up first. They didn't have that kind of time. On one street, a car turned onto the street when they were thirty feet from the intersection. The other car refused to back up. Cots kept advancing on the car, but the driver was stubborn. However, Cots had the larger vehicle and continued to advance. The other driver simply sat where he was, refusing to budge. Cots stopped within two inches of the other car's bumper. The other driver still refused to move.

"Leah, give me your weapon, please," Quinn said.

"Why?"

"I'm going to shoot the son of a Drularian dog."

Leah chose to keep her lemon reamer. Quinn pounded the dashboard in frustration.

"Push him out of the way," Quinn said.

Cots eased off the brake and they felt the big van's bumper tap the car in front of the them. Still, the man didn't put his car into reverse. Cots eased off the brake again. This time, the van managed to move the car an inch or so backward. When the man stepped out of his car to inspect the damage, Cots pushed the smaller car back into a snowbank. The man drew a weapon and advanced on the van. He was halted in his tracks when he recognized the police badge that Leah was holding against the glass next to Cots.

The man retreated to his car and waited until the van passed before he gunned his car and fishtailed down the street and into another snowbank.

"Did we get the stupid asshole's license plate?" Quinn asked.

"Sure did," Cots said.

"Unfortunately, we can't call it in," Leah said.

"Why not?" Quinn demanded.

"First, we don't have the authority to do that. Second, there isn't a law against being a stupid asshole," Leah said with a smile.

Cots pulled the van over to the sidewalk when they were four blocks from the museum. Quinn and Leah got out. Peony moved into the passenger seat without having to get out of the warm van. Leah and Quinn would walk the rest of the way. They gave Cots a ten-minute head start by stepping into a coffee shop and getting the largest coffees they could buy. The sidewalks were cleared of both snow and people. They seemed to be the only people on foot. Leah readily understood why only fools were out of doors. Adding misery to the cold was the wind whistling down the corridors formed by the tall buildings on either side of the street creating a wind tunnel. The wind had to have dropped the wind chill factor to minus fifty degrees, or at least that's what it felt like. As they hurried down the four blocks toward the museum, Leah thought about the state of her marriage. She wasn't one to second-guess herself, but now she wondered if it would have been smarter to have brought Cots with her instead of Quinn. Or if the meeting wasn't one of her dumbest ideas ever.

When they arrived in front of the museum, Leah glanced at the museum parking lot. It was empty. She wondered where Grandini and her people had parked. There weren't that many cars on the street, and Leah spotted their van a half block up the street. Cots had parked at a meter. If they had to flee for their lives, his choice of parking spots was perfect—easy access for Quinn and Leah and a quick getaway.

They went up the stairs, finished their coffees, and threw the containers into the recycler beside the museum doors. *Best to have both hands free.* As they entered the warmth of the museum, a fast look around told them that they were some of the few to brave the elements to visit the museum. Leah wondered why the museum even stayed open on a day like today. She saw two men standing ten feet away from one another, but it was clear they were together because they both looked out of place and they kept throwing each other glances. They were still bundled up as if they were outside. Leah was glad they weren't the brightest mob boys since they'd have difficulty accessing their weapons, regardless of where they were hidden. Their thick gloves would make handling a gun impossible. Their heavy boots would slow them down, too. While she didn't completely rule them out as possible threats, she demoted them down the ladder by several rungs. She wondered how many other men Grandini had brought with her after agreeing that she and Leah would only bring one person each. Apparently, the rules didn't apply to mob bosses.

A man stepped out of the shadows and approached them. He had removed his outer clothing and was dressed in an expensive navy blue suit, pale pink shirt, and a navy tie. He wore loafers, and his hair was slicked straight back with so much styling gunk it looked greasy. It was his eyes that troubled Leah, though. He had the dead eyes of one of those giant sharks that the museum had hanging from the ceiling near something called a whale. The placard near the shark explained that the fish was a man-eater and would attack anything that moved. Everything about this man exuded the same kind of danger.

"Devarian?" the man asked as he ran his eyes over Quinn.

"Yes." Quinn looked as calm as though she'd just agreed it was cold outside.

"Ms. Grandini is expecting you."

He spoke as if Grandini owned the museum. Maybe she did. The man had barely looked at Leah and didn't speak to her.

"This way, please," the man told Quinn. He led them to a door near the visitors' desk. "You can go in," he told Quinn.

When Leah started to follow Quinn into the office, the man stepped in front of her.

"Not you. Just her," he said, nodding toward Quinn.

Before there could be a confrontation between the man and Leah, Quinn said, "She's going in or I'm not. Explain that to your boss."

"My orders are explicit."

Quinn turned around and headed for the front door. Leah fell in beside her. In a way, Leah was glad the meeting was canceled by the stubbornness of one of Grandini's goons.

"Quinn," a voice behind them called.

"Stephanie," Quinn murmured to Leah.

Quinn stopped and turned around, but not before Leah caught the smile of pleasure that flitted across Quinn's face, though it was quickly hidden. Her stomach lurched and she swallowed the bile in her throat. She knew that look well, and what it meant.

The woman was beautiful. She had high cheekbones and dimples. Her blond hair was too blond not to be the work of her stylist. Her makeup was expertly applied. She oozed confidence, power, and sex appeal. Leah couldn't keep her mind from going back to Cots's words that Grandini thought Leah had "stolen" Quinn from her. *Is it any wonder Quinn is attracted to her?* Leah felt decidedly at a disadvantage.

Grandini started across the marble floor toward them. Quinn took a conciliatory step toward her, giving Leah a moment to study the lady mobster.

Grandini wore a navy suit, but hers was obviously tailored for her. She had on a white silk shirt with a stand-up collar. She wore her hair pulled back into a ponytail tied at the neck. Her blue eyes first inspected Quinn and then turned to Leah. Leah watched as Grandini looked her up and down like a shark assessing her next meal.

"Lieutenant Samuels, I'm Stephanie Grandini. Thank you for agreeing to meet here. Did you have much trouble getting through the streets?" she asked as if they were meeting to discuss a legitimate business deal. *Damnation, that voice is sexy as hell.*

"I appreciate your agreeing to meet with me," Leah said. Chitchat, even with mobsters, still wasn't her strong suit.

"Why don't we adjourn to the office? I've got a pot of coffee there."

Grandini didn't wait to see if they would agree to do that. She turned and walked toward the office. Leah watched the ponytail sway gently back and forth in rhythm with her tight ass as she walked. Leah didn't dare look at Quinn for fear of what she would see on her face. *Drude, I hope I get to arrest this woman.*

"Coffee?" Grandini asked when they were in the office.

Both Leah and Quinn declined. Leah wondered if Grandini thought it was because they thought the coffee was poisoned. *Now you're being silly. But anything is possible these days.*

Grandini poured herself a cup. She sat sipping it as she watched them.

"You called this meeting," she finally said to Leah. "It's a shame about Bishop Cohane. Is that why you're here?"

"This was slipped under my door this morning," she said,

ignoring Grandini's question and sliding a copy of the note across the table.

Leah studied Grandini as she began reading the note. Almost immediately, her left eyebrow slowly rose. When Grandini looked up from the note, she cut her eyes to Quinn then said to Leah, "Do you think I sent this note to you?"

"Ms. Grandini, I don't know anything about you except what's in this note. So I don't have a clue whether you had this note delivered to my door, or if someone is genuinely pointing the finger at you. However, it would be logical if you wanted me to know you're sleeping with my wife. A kind of simple opportunity, really. Immature game-playing, but an opportunity nonetheless." Leah hoped Grandini would be so outraged, she would say something incriminating.

"Lieutenant, if I'd wanted you to know I'm fucking your wife, I would have told you myself. I wouldn't slip an anonymous note under your door." She smiled, but it didn't reach her cold blue eyes.

"Much more important to me than you fucking Quinn is the note implicating you in the murder of Bishop Cohane. What can you tell me about that?" Leah asked, aware that Grandini knew the bishop had died in the park murders and that her source for that information could only be one person, and she was sitting in the chair next to hers.

"You don't really think I would admit or deny complicity in the murder of the bishop to the detective investigating the murder, do you?"

"Well, denying it would make sense, if you didn't have anything to do with it," Leah said wryly. "Who would want to implicate you in the murder of the bishop?"

"Lieutenant, is my name anywhere on your fancy murder board at the condo? No? Since it's not, why are you here?"

"I was curious to see if you knew who hated you enough to implicate you in a high-profile murder." She'd known before leaving the condo she probably wouldn't have much time with

Grandini, and she knew Grandini was too smart to implicate herself. All the other questions she had about her relationship with Quinn wouldn't be answered in her lifetime.

"I have no idea who would do that. I'll let you know when I find out." Grandini stood up, signaling the meeting was over. She held out her hand to Leah and said, "It was nice meeting you, Lieutenant."

Leah shook the mobster's hand knowing there was something in Grandini's voice that made Leah feel like she'd been bested by her. She'd have to go over every word spoken to figure out what Grandini thought she'd accomplished.

Grandini next held her hand out to Quinn. "It is nice to see you again, Quinn."

Leah noted Grandini's use of the present tense and the change of tone from arrogant and professional to something softer and sexier. Again, her stomach clenched and she felt a headache coming on.

Once Quinn and Leah were outside the museum, Leah said, "Cots, we'll meet you where you dropped us off. I don't want them knowing about the van."

"Assuming, of course, that they don't already know about it," Cots murmured into Leah's earpiece.

They didn't wait to see Cots drive slowly away from the museum in the opposite direction they were walking. They turned into the wind and headed for the rendezvous point. The wind whipped their words away as soon as they were spoken, making conversation impossible. Which was fine with Leah. She didn't know who she was angrier with—Quinn or Grandini—or both equally. The only thing she'd gotten out of that meeting was that Cots had been right about the two women fucking, and Quinn was almost assuredly providing Grandini information about her murder investigation.

Once inside the warmth of the van with Peony in the driver's seat, Leah unwrapped the scarf from her nose and mouth, and asked Cots, "Were you able to get the conversation?"

"No. They had jamming devices set up in the room you were in. I couldn't overcome them. Did she admit to anything juicy?"

"The only thing she admitted was that she and Quinn are fucking." The second that was out of her mouth, she regretted having said it. *I need to get a grip on my emotions. They cannot be allowed to rule my thinking about this case.* There was dead silence in the van. Quinn didn't say a word, but Leah could sense the tension strumming through her. Quinn's lover had outed her without batting an eyelash. She glanced at Quinn. Her body language confirmed the tension, and it also told her Quinn was furious, but whether at her or Grandini, she had no way of knowing.

Leah remained silent for the rest of the trip home, mulling over the meeting, what was said, and what wasn't said. She was trying very hard not to punch Quinn in the nose for her lying, cheating ways.

"Cots, pull over. Now," Leah said with some urgency. When the van came to a stop she stepped out and barely got to the nearest snowbank before she threw up. She took a handful of snow and wiped her mouth.

No one said anything to her when she got back in the van. Quinn reached over to take her hand, but Leah jerked it way. She didn't want, or need, Quinn's sympathy or pity.

Back in their condo, they shed their outerwear and hung it in the closet. Leah gave the citrus reamer laser gun to Cots while Peony put her non-police-issued weapon in the safe beside the closet. Leah didn't ask Cots for his personal weapon because she assumed he wouldn't give it up.

"I put the coffeemaker on a timer and there should be a full pot if anyone's interested," Cots told them.

"Coffee's not my favorite drink, but I'll drink anything that's hot, including car sludge," Peony told them as she bounced up and down trying to get warm.

"I won't drink car sludge," Quinn told them, "but I will have a cup of coffee."

Leah wasn't interested in adding more acid to her stomach than was already there. She went to the bedroom and went into the bathroom and locked the door. Leah pictured Grandini sipping the coffee in her office. She'd been smug and knowing. And it made Leah sick to her stomach to know Quinn was cheating on her and had been perfectly willing to sit beside her wife and across from her lover. Leah burst into tears and cried until she could get herself under control. She took a washcloth from the linen closet and soaked it in cold water for a few minutes. She folded it and laid it across her eyes, hoping to reduce the appearance that she'd been crying. She didn't want to give Quinn the satisfaction of knowing she'd cried.

There was a knock on the door. "Go away, Quinn," Leah said to the person on the other side of the door.

"It's Cots."

Leah opened the door and let him in. She closed and locked the door behind him.

"I'm so sorry, Leah."

Maybe it was his tone of voice, maybe it was because he was a friend, or maybe it was because her emotions were raw and exposed. Whatever the reason, when he pulled her gently toward him, she didn't fight him. She let him hold her and burst into tears again. When she was once again in control, she stepped back.

"You need to understand that Stephanie is a malicious woman. I'd bet everything I own that she sent the note to you because she wanted to hurt you and hurt you badly. She knew there will be no evidence leading to her, so her motivation for sending it was vindictiveness and jealousy."

"Thanks, Cots. It doesn't make Quinn's betrayal any less painful, but it does explain a lot."

"Let's go get a cup of coffee and get back to work," he said with a gentle smile.

Leah was as much surprised at Cots's behavior as she was of her own. She realized that his gesture of compassion eased her pain just a little, and for that she was grateful, and she'd remember it for the rest of her life.

Leah got herself a cup of coffee, but instead of joining the others in the secure room, Leah stood in front of the living room windows and watched it snow. Not for the first time, she wished her ancestors and the ancestors of every other human on the planet had listened to their scientists about global warming. While current scientists were reluctant to call what they were experiencing an ice age, people on the street knew enough to call it that. There was nothing normal about nine-month winters with temperatures a bone-chilling minus fifty on the worst days. The Chinese were the first to inadvertently sound a warning about cooling temperatures when the government, in 2010, issued a warning to their elderly not to put on too many coats lest they fall down and not be able to get up again. Smug Westerners had thought the warning so amusing. The New American governments had been issuing the same warning to their own elderly every winter for decades.

Leah mentally shook her head to get it back into the game and the problem at hand—who had killed the bishop and why? Who were the other people in the field? Was there any connection between the field and the bombings, or was she seeing something that simply wasn't there? She was becoming frustrated because she wasn't able to find the answers to a single question. At this point, she'd settle for a solid lead to somewhere other than a dead end.

Leah went looking for her pad of paper and a pen. Maybe if she wrote down what she knew, she'd see something she'd missed by having everything on the murder boards. She found her paper and pens on her dresser in the bedroom.

She took the goodies back to her chair in front of the large windows in the living room. Out of habit, she glanced up and down the street to see if she spotted anything or anyone out of place. She didn't. She sat in her chair and thought about what she wanted to write down—what she knew or what she didn't know. What she didn't know would be a much longer list than what she really knew.

Under the heading of Don't Know, she wrote:

1. cause of death of Bishop and the other victims
2. killer(s)
3. motive
4. number of victims and identities
5. who commissioned bombings of the Forty-fourth and crime lab

Leah stopped and looked at what she had written. Without the answers to at least one of those five fundamental questions, she'd have no chance to solve anything. *What am I missing?*

She decided to start with motive. What could be the possible motives for Bishop Cohane?

She got up from her chair and went to the secure room.

"I could use your help. Cots, did we run the financials on the bishop?"

"Yeah, we did."

"Bring them with you, please."

After both Cots and Peony joined Leah in the living room, she said, "I'm trying to figure out what the possible motives might be for killing the bishop. Cots, did anything stand out in his financials? Did he owe anyone money, was he being blackmailed, was he living beyond his means, any indication of an alcohol or drug addiction?"

"No to all your questions. His financials had no red flags. He was paid a substantial salary. The bishop was unmarried. He lived in the archdiocese's mansion and he had a vacation home as well, but it doesn't have a mortgage attached to it. The other research turned up nothing that would motivate someone to kill him."

"Then what is the motive for murdering him?" Leah asked.

There was no answer to her question. Then an idea began forming in Leah's mind. "This is probably far fetched, but what if there's no motive because he wasn't the intended victim?" she asked.

The others sat thinking about what she'd said.

"That could make sense," Cots said.

"What if he was simply at the wrong place at the wrong time?" Leah asked, glad to be brainstorming with her team. *This is the way we'll begin to close in on something that might actually lead us to the killer and the identities of the other victims.*

"Or he happened upon something that he shouldn't have?" Peony asked.

"I wouldn't think that was possible, Peony," Cots said gently.

"Why?"

"The coroner believes that the murders happened between midnight and two in the morning. What would an old religious man be doing out at that hour and in that part of town? He didn't live anywhere near the killing field. He was there because he'd been invited, told to be there, or taken there," Cots said.

"Well, then he couldn't have been an unintended victim either," Peony said.

"Explain," Leah said.

"If he wasn't the intended victim and he wasn't there by accident, then he was there on purpose. We just have to figure out why."

"Are there possibilities for why he was there on purpose?" Leah asked.

The others were silent.

"I can come up with several scenarios, but none of them make any sense when I think them through," Cots said.

"What are the possibilities for what was happening in that field that would get an elderly religious man out of his bed and in that field at midnight?" Leah asked.

"On a frigidly cold and snowy night," Peony added.

"Does the date have any significance?" Leah asked.

"Oh! Wow! Wait a second," Peony said. "Give me a minute."

Peony left them sitting there while she ran back to the secure room. She returned with her computer in hand and began rapidly typing.

"Peony?" Leah asked.

"A moment more," Peony said.

Leah and Cots waited.

Finally, Peony nodded. And then nodded again.

"Tell us." Cots leaned forward, unable to wait any longer.

Peony looked up from her computer. Indecision was written all over her face.

"It's all right," Leah said. "At this stage, anything will help."

"Well," Peony began tentatively, "on the night in question, there was a full moon. We couldn't see it because of the snow clouds, but it was there." Peony paused.

"Go on." Leah was amused at how tentative Peony was being after having spent three days acting like a tough cop.

"On Xing, there is a growing movement, or reemergence, of Wicca."

"Wicca?" Leah and Cots asked in unison.

"Covens, if you will," Peony said, looking at them. When Leah shrugged and Cots just shook his head, she nodded. "All right, let me start at a more basic level." Peony sat back and thought for a moment, and then began again. "A coven is the name used to describe a gathering of witches. In popular culture, these people are called Wiccans and they are followers of a neo-pagan religion called Wicca. The practitioners believe in witches and witchcraft. Most covens have thirteen members who all call themselves witches. The coven is led by a high priestess. Often, their meetings are held out of doors when there is a full moon, usually in open fields or groves. As an aside, the first recorded use of the word 'coven' being applied to witches was in 1662 during a trial of a witch named Isobel Gowdie."

"I have to ask," Cots said when Peony paused, "how do you know so much about this subject?"

"As I said, there's a huge resurgence of the Wicca religion on my home world."

"And? That doesn't mean you'd know so much," Cots said.

Peony blushed slightly. "And my older sister, Isobel, joined a coven two years before I came here. She shared what she was learning with me."

"So your theory is that the, what did you call them?" Leah paused.

"Coven of witches." Peony smiled.

"A coven of witches was meeting in the killing field. The bishop shows up. Then the killer, or killers, descend on them, kill all fourteen people, and chop them up. And they inadvertently leave behind a piece of a hand to be identified. That's your theory?"

"In a nutshell," Peony said.

"Not bad, Detective, not bad. So far that makes more sense than anything else we've come up with."

Peony beamed at Leah's praise.

"Now, tell me why the bishop showed up in that field." The concept was incredibly far fetched, but with nothing else to go on, she was willing to run with it.

"And why the bishop's hand was found, but nothing of the others," Cots added.

"Someone wanted the bishop to be found there." Quinn leaned against the doorway.

Leah ignored her.

Quinn looked like she wanted to say something to Leah but instead said, "They wanted people to believe he wasn't as holy as he seemed?"

"The reason we were given the hand is what we need to figure out. In the meantime, we'll use Peony's coven theory as our working theory without stopping our search for other plausible theories." Leah paused. "Try this on for size, too. The hand wasn't left behind on purpose at all. Maybe leaving it behind was an accident and the killers simply didn't notice it."

Leah knew they wouldn't find any more plausible theory now that they'd debunked their theories that Grandini was somehow involved and/or the bishop was somehow crooked. She would keep looking at any alternative theory that came their way, but this one seemed like a good one.

"Let's call it a night, but don't stop thinking about Peony's theory. It's a good one," Leah said.

Peony grinned broadly at Leah's praise.

As she was picking up her stuff, Leah said, "I'm off to bed. Tomorrow's Sunday. Everyone sleep in. I'll see you at eight," Leah said with a straight face.

"You call that sleeping in?" Cots groaned and slumped in his seat.

"Oh, okay. We'll get started when we get started."

In their bedroom, Quinn said, "We need to talk to clear the air."

"No, we don't. I think the air is clear enough to see that you're a lying, cheating bitch."

"Leah, please. Let's talk this through." Her voice had a pleading tone. Almost.

"Tell me the truth. Right now, Quinn. How long have you and Grandini been fucking this time?" Leah wanted to hear Quinn admit she was cheating.

Quinn stared at her for a few seconds before she finally answered. "Two years."

Suddenly, Leah really didn't give a shit how long Quinn had been betraying her with Grandini. It didn't matter. The damage was done; there was no way Quinn could ever undo that.

There were questions, things she wanted to know, yes. But she couldn't handle the answers right now. "Quinn, there's really nothing to talk about. I think you should sleep elsewhere."

"What does that mean? You want me to leave?"

"Either you leave or I'll move my investigation somewhere else."

"I want to explain why I started seeing Stephanie again. I

thought I could get valuable information for you. Like an uncover cop."

"For two years? On cases I wasn't working? Come on, Quinn, spin your story any way you want. We're through. I told you in the beginning, one of the two things I would not tolerate was infidelity. Now leave."

"I'll give you a few days to come to your senses. Then we'll have a nice dinner out and talk through this."

Leah turned her back on Quinn, went into the bathroom, and slammed the bathroom door so hard it probably awoke residents across the street from them. *That was childish, but it sure as hell felt good. Anyway, it was better than punching her.*

When she exited the bathroom later, Quinn wasn't in the bedroom, much to her relief. Just the thought of "talking it out" with Quinn made Leah nauseous. In a rage, she picked up the photograph of her and Quinn on their wedding day that Quinn kept on her bedside table. She threw it across the room at the door. *Well, that felt good.* She picked up the photo and tried to straighten the frame but could do nothing about the broken glass. She dropped it down the recycling chute in the bathroom. She lay on the bed, still fully clothed, and eventually fell into a troubled, anxious sleep, full of dreams of being chased and falling.

CHAPTER ELEVEN

The next morning, Leah awoke at six. Instead of leaping out of bed, though, she lay snuggled beneath the warmth of the electric blanket Quinn had brought from their apartment and added to their bed the night before. She missed Quinn being tucked against her back with her arm holding her tight. Leah loved those moments when her world felt bright and new and full of possibilities before the ugliness of her day-to-day world intruded. She was both pissed off and devastated by Quinn's behavior. *What else don't I know about Quinn? And does any of it really matter?* She knew she'd miss living with Quinn. It had been easy, perhaps too easy, but easy nevertheless. How could it not be easy when they only spent a few hours of every day together because of their insane working lives? Maybe if she'd looked closer at Quinn, she might have seen her for what she now knew she was—untrustworthy, manipulative, and cheating. Maybe somewhere down the line, they could be friends. But if Quinn was colluding with mobsters as she now knew she was, she wouldn't want to be friends with a cop. *Nor would this cop want to be friends with a possible felon.*

She turned her mind to the case. She wondered whether the case would have been solved by now if she weren't holed up in this condo. No, she decided, if anything, she would be further away from resolution. She had better equipment here, she didn't have a captain breathing down her neck to solve the controversial case, and she didn't have a team of people trying to ensure their pet theory won the day. Granted, it might have helped to have more bodies doing the scut work of canvasing the neighborhood around the park to see if anyone had seen or heard anything. What had helped, she had to admit, was that the bombings had dominated the news cycles for as long as they had, and that those cases had undoubtedly been assigned to other detectives. And the media had moved on to topics that didn't have as much mystery surrounding them and upon which they could pontificate. She wondered whether she should tell the new commissioner she was alive and well. *Not today.* She also wondered if anyone had been assigned the killing field case when it had been presumed she was dead, or if all attention had been turned to the bombings. *Where are they with the cases? What if they have information I don't, and I'm just spinning my wheels out here alone?* The questions were unsettling.

Leah heard someone in the kitchen. She slid out of bed and headed to the shower. After she dressed, she went to the kitchen, where someone, probably Cots, had made a pot of coffee. Cots had apparently accepted coffee duty, which was fine with her. She automatically fixed two mugs of coffee, one with cream and three teaspoons of sugar for Quinn, and one black for her. When she realized what she had done, she poured Quinn's coffee down the drain. *I wish I didn't know about what Quinn did with Grandini. I need some time to wrap my mind around what she's done, time I won't have until the killing field murders are solved.*

Leah took her mug into the living room and activated the murder board. As she sat staring at the various pieces of information on the board, she sipped her coffee. *I wonder why I never liked Cots before now. I really like the guy. He's kind, gentle, funny every once in a while, a wizard at searching out the details of people's lives, and he occasionally breaks the law. I still don't think he's only Quinn's bodyguard, and if he is, he's underemployed. But they're connected somehow, I just don't know how.* Yet again, she had to bring her mind to bear on the case and not wander down another dead-end lane.

After they'd had breakfast, and with mugs of coffee in hand, they gathered in the living room to return to the investigation. Everyone looked rested and a little brighter.

"We're working on the theory Peony brought up about Wicca, and on the possibility that it has spread from Xing to here, both of which are totally unsupported, but we're going to see where it takes us anyway. Can we be sure there was a coven meeting in the field that night?" Leah asked.

"Boss, I know there are covens here. Several, in fact. When I arrived, I was contacted by three of them to join thanks to my sister. I don't know if there was a coven meeting that night, but I can find out," Peony said. "I'll call one of the Wiccans who contacted me."

"Do it. Excluding the bishop from our thinking for a moment, and with thirteen women killed, assuming that was the coven number and Scotty's numbers are wrong, you would have thought that someone's family would have come forward to report their loved one missing, wouldn't you?" Leah hated the amount of assumption in play. "You did say the covens are made up of thirteen women, didn't you?"

"Yeah, for the most part covens are women. There may be an occasional male, but they don't stay around. Maybe loved ones did report them missing. They would have, in all probability, gone to the precinct closest to their homes. And since Taconic Park where the, uh, bodies were found is practically in the center of the Forty-fourth's precinct, it stands to reason that at least some, if not all, of the women lived within the precinct. So any reports of missing persons might have been lost in the bombing, particularly if the receiving officer didn't input the information into the computer fast enough." Peony was on a roll. "Certainly not all of them would have gone to the Forty-fourth. Some may have chosen to deal with their local cops, if they didn't know their family member was in a coven at all, for instance. Their missing persons reports could be spread over several precincts with no way of tying them together because there is no known common denominator."

"Cots, can you check that out? See if there were any missing persons reports on the main computers. We wouldn't have accepted any reports for forty-eight hours, so start there. Also, compile a list of women reported missing the night of the murders at any precinct."

"Right," Cots said as he left the living room to go to the secure room.

"Did anyone talk to the bishop's family?" Leah asked Peony.

"The bishop was unmarried but has a sister. I talked to her on the phone, and she told me when she'd last heard from him. I didn't ask a lot of questions because we'd planned on seeing her in person. We never got a chance to do that, though," Peony said. "So the family doesn't know for sure he's dead."

"Neither do we," Leah told her.

"Didn't Scotty identify the bishop through DNA from the partial hand?" Peony asked.

"He identified a partial *hand* as belonging to the bishop," Leah said. "And he wasn't ready to say for sure it was the bishop."

"Since everyone in the field was chopped up, we might not have declared them dead even if we were still at the precinct house, right?" Peony asked.

"Right. Aside from a partial hand, we don't have any conclusive evidence the bishop was in the field and was killed there. He might be out there, alive, and missing a piece of his hand. So we'd hold off telling the family he's dead until we can unequivocally say he died and how. Yes, we think he's dead and his body was in that field, among the others. But we can't say it for certain."

"Do you have a name of anyone in the bishop's office?" Leah asked Peony.

"His housekeeper mentioned his personal assistant."

"Call the bishop's office and see if you can get me an appointment to meet with her. Somewhere away from his office."

"A secret meet?"

"Yeah."

"Damn, I love this clandestine stuff," Peony said with a smile.

"Set up the meet."

"Yes, ma'am."

Peony left the living room for the electronics room, leaving Leah alone. *We may be on to something. It still feels a little far fetched, but at least we're not sitting around with nothing to do but wait. And my mind doesn't have to be focused on Quinn every second.*

Cots returned with his computer in hand.

"I've found one hundred sixteen women who were reported missing two days after the killings."

"Can we eliminate any of them?" Leah asked.

"We can't do it by age, since age isn't a requisite for being a witch. I concentrated on the women so we can narrow our field," Cots said.

"I spoke to a couple of Wiccans and they told me there were at least three meetings scheduled for that night, including a Dianic coven made up entirely of women. Unfortunately, she couldn't tell me where they were meeting," Peony said.

"Good. What about location? On that particular night, would women from the outskirts of the city come through a blizzard to attend a coven meeting out of doors?" Leah asked.

"Maybe not," Peony said. "If we search for lists of local covens, we might be able to cross-check the missing persons list with the coven lists."

"Let me narrow it using that criteria." He typed furiously and then looked up. "We dropped thirty-six women, leaving us with seventy possible victims," Cots said.

"Delete any women staying at hotels or motels. Let's assume people didn't come from out of town," Leah said.

"We're down to fifty."

"Let's drop any women over the age of sixty, since they would be less likely to go out in the middle of a blizzard," Leah said. "How many does that leave us?"

"Thirty-five."

"Drop any female under the age of fifteen. It's not likely their families would allow them to attend a meeting of any kind in the middle of the night," Leah said.

"Right. We're down to twenty-five," Cots told them.

"Okay, drop any girl between the ages of sixteen and eighteen. With a blizzard going on, their parents, too, would be unlikely to allow them out."

"We've got eleven left."

"Great! At last, something we can work with," Leah said.

Cots put the list onto the murder board and sent it to Peony's computer. Several minutes later, she said, "I've got the addresses on those eleven."

"Bring up a map of the city and pinpoint those addresses," Leah said.

It only took a minute for the computer to do as she requested. The map showed the killing field in the center of eleven red dots. It was a clear, undeniable lead, and Leah let it sink in.

"So covens are organized by neighborhoods?" Leah asked Peony.

"It depends on whether the witches live in a rural or city environment. A city might have dozens of covens, whereas a more remote area might only have one but draw on a wider area."

"After we meet with the bishop's personal assistant, we'll go visit some of these families and see if we can figure out if their daughters were in a coven."

"Does that mean a road trip?" Peony asked hopefully.

"Indeed it does," she said.

"For all of us?" Cots asked.

Leah knew she was feeling a bit claustrophobic from having

been stuck inside for so long. The others must be feeling the same way.

Peony dug her phone out of her pocket and thumbed it on. "Yes?"

Leah and Cots sat listening to a one-sided conversation. When Peony broke the connection, she said, "I got you the meet this afternoon at noon."

"Where? Somewhere indoors, I hope," Leah said.

"Yeah, there's a bookstore right outside the bishop's neighborhood with a decent coffee shop. We'll meet there."

"Thanks for arranging the meet," Leah said.

"That's our road trip?" Cots asked, clearly disappointed.

"Not all of it. We're also going to interview some families of missing women from the neighborhoods surrounding the park. We probably won't get to all of them today, but we'll have a good start and might get some more information to add to our almost nonexistent murder book."

Every cop kept a murder book on every case she caught. It contained transcriptions of interviews, photos, reports from others, like the ME, the cop's notes on the case, including speculations, guesses, and anyone they suspected but couldn't implicate in the murder. Some of the information was put on the electronic murder board, but not the personal stuff, like the cop's assessment of an interviewee, his speculations, and his gut feelings.

Thus far, Leah's murder book consisted of the crime lab's preliminary reports, the transcriptions of the telephone interviews with the bishop's family, photos of the bishop, and precious little more. After this afternoon's interviews, it would be fattened by a lot more information, she hoped. Or this could be a wild-goose chase and they'd still have nothing.

As they prepared for their mini road trip, Leah got out a second heavy winter coat, gloves, scarf, and an unattractive but warm hat. When Peony came to the door so layered up that she looked like a second-grader in her school play about large vegetables, Leah pointed at the pile of clothing she had removed from the coat closet.

"I'm fine," Peony told her.

"You're not fine. Show me your weapon."

By the time Peony took off her gloves and dug through her layers of clothing to reach her gun, Leah had put her harness on, removed her weapon, and pointed it at Peony.

"Point taken. But—" Peony said.

"You can either wear this stuff," Leah said, interrupting Peony and motioning at the pile of clothes, "or stay here."

"I'll wear the warm stuff." Peony began peeling clothes off one layer at a time.

They decided only Peony and Leah would be pounding the pavement from house to house. Cots would stay in the van and monitor them. Before leaving the condo, Leah checked the weather report. It was going to be a sunny morning with a high for the day of minus twenty-six. *Positively balmy.* The afternoon would turn ugly, though. Another blizzard was expected to descend on the city by midafternoon.

"Change of plans. We'll get in as many interviews as we can this morning, before the meeting with the bishop's assistant, and we'll do a couple after if we have time. We'll need to be back before three this afternoon. I don't want to be out when the blizzard storms into town," Leah said.

As Cots got them under way, Peony's phone rang. Her conversation consisted of one "I see" and one "I understand." She ended it by saying, "I'll call later today to reschedule." After keying off her phone, Peony said, "The meet with the bishop's assistant is postponed. Something came up at the archdiocese."

"Okay," Leah said, only slightly disappointed. She really wanted to interview the parents of the missing young women. "Cots, take us to the first house on the list."

Cots drove past the house and parked the van. Leah and Peony got out and walked up to the house. It was a well-kept home that looked similar to every other house in the neighborhood. Leah bet that in the summer, the owners had a nicely manicured lawn and maybe even a few flowers in a bed by the porch, and allowed herself to feel a little envious of the people living here.

Leah rang the doorbell and waited. She could hear noises inside, but no one came to the door, so she rang the doorbell a second time.

The woman who opened the door wore a well-worn robe and slippers. Her hair was lank and greasy looking. She looked like she hadn't slept in weeks. There were dark circles covering the bags beneath her eyes.

"Yes?" the woman asked.

"Mrs. Gabrielle?" Leah asked.

"Yes?"

"We're with the police. I'd like to ask you a few questions about your missing daughter."

"It's about time," the woman murmured as she stepped aside to let them enter.

The living room, unlike its owner, was neat and clean. Leah glanced around and knew this was a woman who liked order in her life. There didn't seem to be anything askew. Like Leah's mother, this woman knew the "there is a place for everything and everything in its place" rule of housekeeping. Leah noticed a row of photographs on the mantel over the fireplace. She moved to the fireplace to look at the photographs.

"Is this your daughter?"

"Yes, that's my Marian." Her voice was raspy, like she'd been crying nonstop for a very long time.

"Pretty name," Peony said gently.

"Thank you. When I was ten, I read about a scoundrel named Robin Hood and the love of his life, Marian. I fell in love with the name and promised myself to name my oldest child Marian," the woman said with a small smile.

Leah nodded at Peony to keep going while she inanely wondered what the woman would have done if her eldest child had been a boy. *Named him Marion, perhaps?*

"Mrs. Gabrielle, how old is your daughter?" Peony asked.

"She's only twenty," she told them with tears in her voice.

"Does she live at home?"

"Yes. And attends City University. She wants to be a pediatrician."

"You must be proud."

Marian's mother could only nod.

"Mrs. Gabrielle, what can you tell us about the night your daughter went missing?"

"Well, she told me she had to attend a meeting that night. I didn't want her to go out. It was a freezing night. I had a really bad feeling, so I asked her to stay home. She told me she couldn't. It was important she be at the meeting."

"Did she say why?" Peony asked.

"No. I don't think I asked her why, though."

"What time did she leave the house, do you remember?"

"About ten. I think the ten o'clock news on Channel 245 had just come on."

"Did she say anything about where the meeting was going to be held?"

Mrs. Gabrielle paused as she thought back to that awful night. "No."

"Was that unusual?" Peony asked.

"She almost always told me where she was going and when she thought she'd be home. Then, if she was going to be late, she'd always call."

"You said 'almost always.' Were there other times she didn't tell you where she'd be?"

Again, Mrs. Gabrielle paused to think. "About a year ago, for the first time ever, she forgot to tell me where she was going. I think it became a once-a-month thing to forget to tell me."

"Was it always on the same day of the month?" Peony asked.

"Now that you mention it, no. It seemed to vary from month to month."

"Do you remember when last month's meeting was?"

Mrs. Gabrielle had to think about it for a minute. "No, I don't. Is it important?"

"Not really. I just need to know if she had a routine."

Leah was surprised and pleased that Peony knew they needed to verify their theory that the women had been at a coven meeting the night they died. One way of doing that was to confirm the meetings the parents could remember were always on the night of a full moon.

"Did your daughter belong to any clubs, organizations, or groups?"

"She belonged to two or three campus groups, if that's what you mean. She was a member of our church even though she seldom attended once she started at the university."

"What church do you attend?"

"We attend the archdiocese church over on Church Street."

"You can't think of any other groups she belonged to?"

"No, I can't."

"Did she ever mention the word 'coven' to you?" Leah asked.

"As in witch's coven?" Mrs. Gabrielle asked, her expression bemused.

"Yes."

"No. She would have known we'd be opposed to such a thing." She drew her robe tighter around her, as though to protect herself. "Why do you ask about covens? I know we, or any other parent, wouldn't allow their child to join such a thing."

"We?" Peony asked, thus avoiding answering the question about covens.

"Her father and I."

"Where is her father?" Leah asked, still looking at the photos.

"He's at work. He stayed home the first day our Marian went missing, but he had to return to work or lose his job."

"Where does he work?"

"At Allied Manufacturing."

"Only another question or two. Do you know if any of her friends went out with her the night she went missing?"

"No. I called her best friend's parents the next morning, but her father said that his daughter had had a sleepover with another friend that night."

"Thank you, Mrs. Gabrielle, you've been quite helpful. Is there a photo I can take with me to help in the investigation of your daughter's disappearance?" Leah asked. "I'll make sure you get it back," she added when she saw the woman frown.

"You can have one of those as long as you promise to return it," Mrs. Gabrielle said, pointing at the photographs on the mantel.

Leah took a photograph where Marian was alone. She was smiling into the camera. She was a pretty young woman with black hair and laughing blue eyes.

Out on the sidewalk in front of the Gabrielle house, Leah said, "Nice work in there. You're a natural. I want you to take the lead on all the interviews."

"Thanks, Boss," Peony said with a grin. "Who's next?"

"Sophie Quincey's parents."

Leah led them past the parked van and across the street to the Quincey house. The interview there went much like the one at the Gabrielle's house. Like Mrs. Gabrielle, Mrs. Quincey didn't know exactly where her daughter had gone the night she went missing, and she said their daughter didn't know Marian.

Afterward, they went farther up the block to Lucia Martinelli's home. The Martinellis' interview didn't give them any new information about the coven or what their daughter was doing the night of the murders. However, they did learn that Marian and Lucia had been friends since kindergarten.

"We'll do two more and then call it a day. I don't like the looks of those clouds rolling in. And the temperature is dropping," Leah said, rubbing her gloved hands together to ward off the cold.

The next house they went to belonged to the family of Grace

Potter. The house, like all the others in this neighborhood, was well cared for, although the Potters' front yard looked like it had many flower beds beneath the snow. The house had an eerie stillness about it.

"Be alert, Peony," Leah said as they climbed the five steps to the porch.

Leah rang the bell. At first, she thought no one was home. Then, she heard footsteps slowly approaching the door. The woman who opened the door was elderly, in her seventies at least. She wore her steel gray hair tied into a ponytail at the nape of her neck. She had on a shapeless dress, socks, and a pair of slippers.

"May I help you?" the woman asked.

"Mrs. Potter?" Leah asked.

"Yes?"

"We're police and have come to talk about the missing person's report you filed on Grace Potter."

She didn't look surprised, nor did she look hopeful. "Do come in. I've just poured myself a cup of tea. Would you like one, dear?"

"Yes, ma'am," Peony answered.

"None for me, thanks," Leah said.

Mrs. Potter shuffled out of the room, giving Leah and Peony a chance to look around the room. Like the other parents, Mrs. Potter had photographs of her daughter on the mantel. Grace was a beautiful young lady.

"Here you are, dear," Mrs. Potter said, handing Peony a cup and saucer. "I took the liberty of adding two sugars and a bit of milk to your tea."

"That's how I like it, ma'am," Peony said.

Leah smiled but stayed quiet. Peony didn't like that much sugar in her tea. She really was good at putting people at ease and thus getting them to answer her questions.

"So did my Grace," the woman said sadly.

"Mrs. Potter, is Grace your daughter?" Peony asked.

"Good gracious, no. She's my youngest granddaughter.

Thank you for asking, though. Just the thought of having a daughter that age makes me feel younger," Mrs. Potter said with another smile.

"Tell us about Grace," Peony said.

"Grace is in her second year at City University. She's studying one of the sciences that I can never remember. Archaeology or astrology, I think. I get those two mixed up."

"Me, too."

"Anyway. She was happy and doing well."

"Did she ever stay out all night without telling you?"

She leaned forward and placed her hand on Peony's leg. "Never. Ever since her mother died, she's been living with me. Grace had a chance to go to another school somewhere off planet, but stayed here to take care of me. We were compatible. I tried not to ask about boys, and she tried not to fuss over me," Mrs. Potter said, smiling at her memories.

A few more questions didn't give them any new information. Leah wanted to get home and warm.

"One last question, Mrs. Potter. Did Grace belong to any groups or organizations?"

"Do you mean other than the ones she belonged to at school?"

Peony nodded, setting her empty teacup on the table.

Mrs. Potter sat thinking for a moment. Leah thought she was trying to make up her mind about whether to tell them the truth. *I've gotten jaded. Now I think even old women are lying to us.*

"Do you mean like the coven?"

"Exactly," Peony said, successfully hiding her surprise and excitement.

"Gracie was following in the footsteps of her maternal ancestors back several generations. They were all witches and all belonged to this coven. The interest in covens and witches skipped my generation. I wanted nothing to do with them. But Grace was fascinated. She joined the coven as soon as she could, at sixteen."

"Do you know if there was a meeting of the coven on the night she disappeared?"

"Of course there was. There was a full moon that night. I didn't want her to go out because of the weather, but she insisted she couldn't miss the meeting."

"Could you tell me if these other girls were members of Grace's coven?" Leah asked her first question as she pulled the photographs of the other girls out of her bag.

"Why yes, they are. These girls grew up together. They've been friends since first grade. In fact, Marian is her best friend," Mrs. Potter said, pointing to Marian's photograph.

"Did you know all these girls were reported missing on the same night as your granddaughter?"

"I knew some of them were maybe missing. I called Marian's house, but she wasn't home and her mother didn't know where she was. A couple of the other parents said their daughters were staying with friends in the city."

"Did you tell the police about the other missing girls?" Peony asked.

"Of course, dear. We even put up posters, but the wind whipped them off the light poles as soon as we put them up. The police told me they couldn't do anything about any missing person for forty-eight hours. If the girls were still missing after the requisite amount of time passed, they would all be assigned to the same detective. But…"

"But what, Mrs. Potter?" Peony asked gently.

"But then that terrible bombing happened. Some of us tried calling so our girls wouldn't be forgotten, but the line was always busy. One of the parents, I don't remember who, even called the commissioner's office and was told they would make sure the case was reassigned. So far, though, we hadn't heard from anyone until you showed up. Do you think it had anything to do with the coven?"

"We're not speculating on anything, Mrs. Potter. It's too soon in the investigation on these girls' whereabouts to speculate." Leah didn't want to give her any false hope, but she finally knew they had something to follow.

"One last question, Mrs. Potter. Do you know if any of the other parents weren't as understanding as you are about their daughters belonging to a coven?" Peony asked.

"I'm not sure they even knew. For instance, since grade school, Alexandra Martin's father was never happy about his daughter's association with the rest of the girls. But whether he even knew about her belonging to the coven is questionable. Alex knew not to tell him everything. Frank, Alex's father, is an unhappy man who takes his woes out on his family, particularly his wife."

As they were leaving the Potter house, Peony handed Mrs. Potter her card. "Please call me if you think of anything else."

"I will, dear. And thank you for coming by. I was beginning to wonder if the police even cared my Gracie was missing. I know they're busy with those terrible bombings, but still…the rest of us need help, too."

"We care, Mrs. Potter, a great deal."

When they were on the sidewalk in front of the Potter house, Leah said, "Alexandra Martin lives across the street, let's talk to her parents and then we'll call it a day."

At Alexandra Martin's house, a man jerked the door open like he was ready for a fight. He was dressed in a dirty T-shirt and dirtier jeans. His feet were bare. He had a paunch hanging obscenely over his belt. His face was the red of a heavy drinker. He'd probably been a weightlifter when he was younger, but now all his muscles had gone to flab. Plus, he smelled of sweat and beer. Leah had come across his type a lot when she'd worked the streets, and she kept a good distance.

"What?" the man demanded belligerently.

"Be careful," Leah murmured under her breath to Peony, who nodded.

"Who is it, Frank?" a woman's voice from inside the house asked.

Frank ignored the question and stared at them with mean little eyes.

"Mr. Martin, we're with the police department and we'd like to ask you a few questions about your daughter, Alexandra," Peony told him.

"Show me some identification."

Leah and Peony pulled out their badges and flashed them at the man.

"Can we come in?" Peony asked.

"I guess," Mr. Martin said as he stood aside.

A woman was standing at the door leading into another room. Leah could see counters and assumed it was the kitchen. When Leah looked at the woman, she lowered her eyes. *I bet Frank beats his wife. I'd love to beat on him before I leave.* She hated bullies of any kind.

The Martins' living room was a mess. Beer cans were amassed on a small table next to what was obviously Mr. Martin's chair in front of an old-fashioned first generation vidscreen. Newspapers littered the floor around the chair. On the coffee table were magazines about guns and hunting. The man was the very epitome of a Luddite, and like others of his ilk, resisted change and technology. Looking around, Leah noticed the rest of the house was as neat as Mrs. Gabrielle's and the others' homes. It was only Mr. Martin's space that looked like a pigsty.

Mr. Martin sat in his chair and leaned back so the leg rest came up. He didn't invite Leah or Peony to sit. Peony sat anyway. Leah wandered over to the mantel to look at the photographs. There was only one photograph of Alexandra, and while she was looking at the camera, she looked scared to death. The rest of the photographs were of Frank dressed as some sort of militia man with other men similarly dressed.

"Mrs. Martin, please join us." Peony motioned toward the couch next to her.

Mrs. Martin darted a scared glance at her husband. He ignored her. She came into the room, and Leah had the sense she was tiptoeing. She sat as far away from Frank as possible on the edge of the chair, as though to ensure she could make a run for it if necessary. Frank said nothing, but his jaw clenched as he stared at his vidscreen.

"Mrs. Martin, how old is Alexandra?" Leah asked, knowing it would piss Frank off that her questions were directed at his wife rather than him.

"She was eighteen," Frank said.

"Nineteen," Mrs. Martin said under her breath.

Leah gave Mrs. Martin a small nod. "When you reported your daughter missing, you said she was nineteen. Which is it, Mr. Martin?"

Frank obviously wasn't used to a woman contradicting him, as his face flushed a deeper shade of red.

"What does it matter?" He glared at Leah.

"Well," Leah said slowly, "you either lied when you reported your daughter missing or you're lying now. I'd like to know which it is."

"So I don't know how old the little whore is," Frank said.

Mrs. Martin reacted to the word "whore" as if she'd been slapped. "Frank, you know that's not true," she said softly.

"Shut up, bitch. No one asked you for your opinion." Frank glared at her.

"Mr. Martin—" Peony said, moving slightly in front of Mrs. Martin as though to shield her.

"Listen, bitch, this is my house and I'll do as I please."

Leah walked over to the end of Frank's chair. She put her boot on the leg rest and slammed it down. Frank was nearly thrown from his chair. He struggled to his feet and came face-to-face with Leah, who stared him down.

"Mrs. Martin, would you like to leave this house?" Leah asked in a voice as cold as the temperature outside the house, without taking her eyes from Frank.

"Yes," Mrs. Martin whispered.

"Don't you dare leave, bitch," Mr. Martin said, not looking away from Leah.

"Take Mrs. Martin out of here, Detective," Leah told Peony.

Peony quickly hurried Mrs. Martin to the coat closet near the front door and helped her get bundled up against the cold. Mrs. Martin didn't say a word, but she was shaking so hard it looked painful.

Frank made a move as if to prevent his wife from leaving but found Leah in his way. When he went to shove Leah aside, he found himself on the floor.

"Get up," she growled at him.

Frank got quickly to his feet. Leah expected him to swing and moved quickly when he did, taking only a glancing blow on her shoulder. She moved a half step back out of range, adrenaline pumping through her. "Assaulting a police officer will get you three to five in the state prison, Frank." She watched the rage build in his expression. "You won't last long when I let it be known you were bested by a woman cop."

"Bitch, I'll kill you."

"You can try, Frank." Leah planted her feet and waited.

He swung at her again. She stepped easily out of his reach. He was breathing hard now. Before he knew what was happening, Leah landed a hard right to his gut and then a left to his face. He fell back into this chair holding his bleeding nose.

"You broke my node," he said incredulously.

"I better be the last woman you hit. If I get even a whiff of your having raised your hand to another woman, I will come back here and finish the job I started. Do you understand?"

Frank stupidly didn't say a word.

"Do. You. Understand?" She wanted to hit him. She wanted

to batter him into the floor and take out every ounce of frustration and anger she'd felt over the last several days on his bloated, ugly face.

When Frank didn't say anything, Leah took a step toward him.

"I understand. I understand," he said quickly, while cowering deeper into his chair.

"Good."

"This was police brutality," he yelled at her retreating back,

"So report me," she said over her shoulder, knowing he didn't know who she was since neither she nor Peony had introduced themselves. Not to mention, he'd never admit a female cop had put him down.

Leah walked out the door. She didn't bother closing it.

CHAPTER TWELVE

Leah returned to the van and got into the passenger seat. Peony and Mrs. Martin were in the second row of seats. Cots asked, "Are you okay?"

"I'm fine. Head out," she told Cots, who'd kept the van running.

Leah glanced back at Mrs. Martin. She looked afraid to move, afraid to talk. Her breathing was rapid. Leah hoped she wasn't having second thoughts about leaving her husband. But when she looked at Leah, the steel in her eyes was clear.

"Can you teach me to do that?" Mrs. Martin asked in a small voice.

"You won't need to know how to do that, Mrs. Martin. Not after today." Leah gave her a quick smile and hoped like hell she wouldn't go back to the bastard.

Leah directed Cots to a house on the other side of the city. While they were on their way, she could hear Peony talking quietly with Mrs. Martin. The kid was a really good interviewer. She had the right combination of hard questions and a sympathetic tone that would elicit responses.

At the women's shelter, Peony got out with Mrs. Martin and went with her into the house.

"You heard?" Leah asked, suddenly exhausted.

"Yeah. I'm surprised you didn't do more than break his 'node,'" Cots said.

"I wanted to. But he's not worth the hassle. I'm just glad we got her out of there."

It took Peony a half hour to get Mrs. Martin checked into the shelter and settled in her room, but there was no conversation to be had in the van, and Leah was too tired to try. By the time Peony returned, it had begun to snow as the promised storm system moved in over the city. As they neared the condo, Cots pulled into the parking lot of the neighborhood grocery store, Mario's Bodega.

"I'll only be a few minutes. I need to restock. The weather reports are saying we could be stuck inside for a few days."

Peony was busy making notes on her computer.

At last, we've got a lead. We'll have to wait until after the storm to interview the other parents, but we can put a few other things in motion in the meantime. When Leah's phone vibrated in her pocket, it startled her. She pulled it from her pocket and checked to see who was calling. It was Quinn. She hit the reject button; she had nothing to say to her.

It actually took Cots twenty minutes to return. Leah watched as the snow came down quicker and the large fluffy snowflakes became smaller and denser. *This is going to be a nasty storm if it hangs around.* She knew they weren't going to go out in this blizzard unless they absolutely had to.

"It's like a zoo in there," Cots said when he returned. "The shelves are nearly empty. Mario can't decide whether to be happy or sad. But I was able to get what we needed." Cots put the bags of groceries in the van beside Peony.

As he climbed into the driver's seat, Leah asked, "How many people did you have to hurt to get everything you wanted?"

"Only one," Cots told her with a smile. "And only because she tried to take the last dozen eggs from my basket." Cots paused. "And because she called me a bitch."

Cots had them quickly back in their parking slot in the warm garage.

"Peony and I'll take the groceries if you'll deal with the equipment," Leah said. She knew he'd put blankets over the equipment as much to hide it as to keep it warm. She understood that irreparable damage would result if the computers were left in the sub-zero weather too long. The heated garage would stay warm enough to protect cars and computers alike, but it didn't hurt to have an abundance of caution in these matters.

Once in the condo, Peony and Leah took the grocery bags into the kitchen and set them down. After removing their outerwear and stowing their weapons, they started putting the groceries away.

"I feel like I'm finally a real detective," Peony said as she put the eggs into the refrigerator. "Thanks, Boss."

"Like I said, Peony, you're a natural. You have a gift few of us have at such an early stage of our careers. It took me forever to learn subtlety, but it seems to easily come to you. I was impressed. Did you learn anything new from Mrs. Martin that we didn't already know?" Leah asked.

"No. She was too shaken to be able to think straight. She told the intake person at the shelter that Frank beat her on a regular basis and terrorized their daughter. He didn't even bother to help the other parents put up flyers and wouldn't talk to the ones who came to their door. And, of course, he wouldn't let his wife out of his sight. While he was at work, she called Mrs. Potter to tell her Alexandra was missing, too. She didn't know anything about covens."

"Good job, Detective."

Leah knew she was laying it on a bit thick, but the young detective deserved the praise. Leah also knew there was a good chance both their careers would be over at the end of this investigation. They'd broken several policies and procedures during the course of this morning alone. Add to that the fact they hadn't reported for duty after the bombing of their precinct, and the commissioner had grounds for dismissal. She would try to take full responsibility for what they were doing but knew Peony would be painted with the same black brush as Leah because she hadn't left the investigation and returned to work.

After she and Peony put away the groceries, Peony went into the secure room to enter her notes on the morning's interviews into the case files on her computer. Leah knew they would show up on the murder board and in the murder book within the half hour.

"Cots, you know Commissioner Robinson, don't you?" Leah asked when he returned to the condo. For some reason, Leah figured that if Quinn had connections in high places, Cots might, too.

"Of course."

"Can you call and get me an appointment for tomorrow morning?"

"I can call, but I don't think I've got the firepower to order her to do anything."

"See what you can do to get us an appointment. We need an arrest warrant and a couple of search warrants." Leah didn't want to go to her captain or the chief of police for the things she needed to close this case. They'd want to know why she hadn't reported in for duty and why she'd been acting alone. She didn't have the time to fight that battle right now. She knew that at the time she'd taken her team and her case off the grid, she'd made the right decision and her bosses had agreed with that decision, but she also knew it might not fly with the chain of command now. She needed to focus on who killed the people in the park and why. After she did that, she'd work with the cops handling the bombing of the precinct house and the crime lab complex to see if there was a connection to her case. If it turned out the cases were connected, then she'd definitely been right to move off-site, and that would be the primary reason she gave to her superiors. If it turned out the cases weren't connected…well, she'd figure that out when the time came.

I wonder if Quinn has the "firepower" to get me an

appointment in the morning? She was damned sure not going to ask her.

Leah felt her phone vibrating in her pocket. She didn't need to pull it to know it was Quinn. While she didn't want to talk to her, she had too many unanswered questions about her and Grandini. Quinn had never said her name in front of Leah until earlier in the week. *Do I really need to know more about Grandini or is it merely morbid curiosity?* She knew Quinn would keep calling or, heaven forbid, come to the condo if she didn't answer her phone. She didn't want a confrontation with Quinn with Cots and Peony in the condo. Better to talk to her on the phone where she wouldn't be tempted to punch her.

With a sigh, she pulled her phone out and speed-dialed Quinn.

"Thanks for calling me back," Quinn said. "We need to talk. Can I come over?"

Technically, since it was Quinn's condo, she didn't need permission to come over. Leah didn't want her there, but she didn't want to go out in the storm, and Quinn might have information that could help her move on, personally and professionally. Hopefully, they could keep it quiet so it didn't impact the other two in the condo. "Yeah, come over."

Quinn didn't mention the lack of enthusiasm in Leah's voice but said, "I'll be right there."

In reality, it took Quinn nearly an hour to reach the condo; Leah spent the time trying to stay focused on the case but failing miserably as she considered the forthcoming discussion.

After Quinn removed her outer clothing, Leah led her into the bedroom. One look at Quinn's expression told her that Quinn expected to get laid. *Never again in this lifetime.* Leah closed the door and turned back to Quinn.

"It's time for you to come clean. No more of me having to pull information from you or find out things when they happen to come up. The truth. Now."

Quinn didn't protest. Instead, she sat on their bed and patted the space beside her for her to sit. Leah stayed standing.

She nodded, looking resigned. "Stephanie and I were together for four years before she took over as head of her family."

Yet another thing we thought we knew but couldn't confirm, and yet Quinn knew this and knew we wanted to know it. "Did you live with her?"

"Yes. We lived here for three years. I asked for the front door key card when she left and she gave it to me. I assumed it was for the front door to this building, but since I didn't check to make sure, it could be to the front door of any building."

"Did you love her?" Leah's chest hurt as the words hit the air.

"Yes. Very much."

"Did she love you?"

"Yes, very much." Quinn stayed completely still, not meeting Leah's eyes.

"But?" Leah waited. "Drude, Quinn. Answer me."

"Her father didn't like me because I'm an alien. I told him about being a Devarian when I asked his permission to marry Stephanie. His answer was immediate and emphatically *no*," Quinn said bitterly. "It was okay to do business with me; it wasn't okay for me to marry his daughter."

She wanted to marry her. Before me, she wanted someone like that. She felt clammy; too hot, too cold. "Why did you ask for his permission and why didn't you ignore the old man?"

"I asked because he was an old-fashioned man who expected such things. I extended that courtesy to him. I was willing to ignore his response, but Stephanie wasn't willing to go against her father. I think she knew she wouldn't win the battle. In the end, she chose her family over me."

"How old were you?"

"I was twenty-nine. Steph was twenty-four."

"Do you still have feelings for her?" Leah already knew the answer but needed to know if she would still lie to her at this stage.

Quinn flinched slightly but looked up. "Yes and no. I have feelings such as one would have for any distant, long-over relationship. I'm no longer in love with her, but there is a fondness there, yes. Each of us has changed a great deal over the years. She's become head of an interstellar crime syndicate, and I have become a successful businesswoman who has to, occasionally, do business with the crime syndicates. I'll admit, it has helped my business prospects that people know I had an association with the Grandini family."

"People who know of the 'association' may think you're still in bed with the family," Leah said. She fought hard to keep her temper in check. Raging at Quinn would change nothing.

"You know I don't care what people say about me."

"I do know that. But I don't have the luxury of not caring what people say about me. You can't be a cop and have people believing you're in the pocket of a crime syndicate."

"I understand. I don't know what to do about that, but I do understand your position and how untenable it might be. I'm sorry I didn't tell you sooner, but if you'd known you wouldn't have been with me."

You're damn straight about that. Quinn didn't sound like she was sorry either. Like most narcissists, she knew what she was supposed to say even if she didn't actually feel the emotion of regret. Leah had seen it in interrogation rooms too many times to count over the years. She knew what no remorse looked like. "What's your connection to Grandini today?"

"I hadn't seen her for three years until yesterday at the museum."

My God, the woman can't stop lying about Grandini. Leah wanted to believe it. Desperately. But she didn't. When Grandini had said point-blank they were sleeping together, Quinn hadn't denied it. And she'd seen the way Quinn had looked at her. Leah knew the truth.

"Are we good?" Quinn asked.

"Seriously? You need to ask that question? Quinn, you've

kept too many things from me for no good reason. You've jeopardized my career, and you've broken faith with me. You've lied to me and, on any number of levels, betrayed me. I have no idea what you told her about our case, and I'm not going to ask because I don't believe you'd tell me the truth. And as for that stunt with the note under the door..." She shook her head, still baffled by it. "I don't know what kind of game the two of you are playing, and to be honest I don't care anymore. So no, we're not good. Not now, never again." Leah turned her back on Quinn. She didn't want to cry in front of her whether they were tears of anger, disappointment, or sadness.

The silence lengthened uncomfortably before Leah sighed and headed for the door, but she paused and turned back to Quinn. "I don't think it's a good idea for you to stay here."

"But I want to be here with the team."

"You're not a member of the team, Quinn. You're not a cop, and you've got no reason to be involved in my case. And even you don't always get what you want. If you insist on staying here, I'll take *my* team to a hotel."

"All right, I'll go. But can we maybe talk some more later?"

"Just go, Quinn," Leah said wearily.

Once Quinn was gone, Leah heaved a big sigh. She tried to figure out how she felt. There were so many emotions—disappointment, betrayal, jealousy, anger, especially anger—swirling around inside her she couldn't put a finger on any one of them and say that was how she felt. Trying to deal with her runaway emotions was exhausting. *I need to get back to something safe to focus my mind on—like the murders in the field.*

CHAPTER THIRTEEN

G ood morning," Leah said as she entered the kitchen the next morning.

"Good morning, Boss," Peony said cheerfully.

Cots mumbled something indiscernible. Leah didn't bother asking what it was he'd said. He was obviously not a morning person.

"We've got another road trip today. Two actually."

"Great. I love road trips. Where are we going?" Peony said.

"At ten thirty, we're having tea with the commissioner, and at two, we're meeting with the bishop's personal assistant."

"Have either of you looked outside yet?" Cots asked.

"No. Why?"

"Go look."

Leah and Peony went to the large windows in the living room.

"How beautiful," Peony murmured like the newcomer she was. It had apparently snowed the entire night. There was no dirty snow to be seen anywhere. The world looked new and shiny white.

Leah was more pessimistic, however. She didn't see the beauty of the scene outside her windows. All she saw was eighteen more inches of new snow on top of the hundred and forty-four inches already on the ground. She also saw the trees swaying and knew the wind chill had to be way, way below zero.

"The good news is they're predicting we'll see sun today," Cots said from behind them.

"Sun. I've barely seen the sun since I got here last fall. I miss the sun," Peony said wistfully, exaggerating only slightly.

"And the bad news?" Leah had to ask.

"They have no idea how long it will take them to get the side streets to the point of being able to drive on them. But the main streets should be cleared in a couple of hours, maybe," Cots said.

"Let's hope so," Leah and Peony said in unison.

"Anyone want breakfast?" Cots asked.

"If you're making pancakes again, I'm in," Peony told him.

"Me, too," Leah agreed.

Leah and Peony joined Cots in the kitchen. "I want to know everything there is to know about Frank Martin. What he does for a living, how often his wife and child ended up in the hospital, who his enemies are. Everything," Leah said.

"May I ask why?" Cots asked.

"The bishop may have simply been in the wrong place at the wrong time, but the killer or killers were there on purpose. What if this isn't anything more than something domestic? That would mean someone who knew one of the coven members may be the killer."

"And since most of the parents didn't know, or said they didn't know, that their daughters were involved in a coven, it could mean one of them was lying to us. I agree Frank Martin could be the one," Peony said.

"Yeah, that's kind of where I was going, too," Leah said.

"It actually makes sense, doesn't it?" Cots asked.

"What do you mean?" Leah asked.

"He's a nasty piece of shit. He thinks his seventeen-year-old daughter is a whore. Who better to do this than someone like him?"

"Before we decide to close the case based on Martin's ugliness, let's find out what the man does for a living, whether he has priors, etc. Let's finish this one by the book and let's be thorough," Leah said.

After the kitchen was cleaned up, they adjourned to the secure room where each of them got onto a computer.

Five minutes later, Peony said, "Got it. You're not going to believe this."

"What?" Leah and Cots said in unison.

"Martin works for the city's Parks and Recreation Department."

"Doing what?" Leah asked.

"He's been in the maintenance department for over nineteen years. And here's where it gets good. He heads up the crew that does tree maintenance," Peony said.

"He maintains the trees?" Cots asked, clearly confused.

"In a matter of speaking. He prunes the trees, takes down dead or diseased trees, and cleans up the branches and limbs blown off during storms."

"Yeah, so? Will you stop teasing us and tell us what's got you so pleased with yourself?" Cots asked.

"He's got a chipper assigned to him by the department," Peony said with a wide grin.

"What's a chipper?" Cots looked at Leah.

"A chipper, Cots, is a machine that you feed limbs and the like into and it chews them up and spits them out in tiny, biodegradable pieces." Leah stared at the murder board, trying to put the new information into place.

"Just like the victims at the killing field," Cots said.

"Exactly," Peony said.

"Remember, let's play this one by the book. We'll need a search warrant to go over his chipper and we need more info on Martin's job. Find out whether Martin used a chipper either the day of or the day after the murders," Leah told them as she left the secure room to go to the living room to adjust her thinking on the case and to figure out what needed to be done next.

This was the first break they'd had in the case, and Leah's gut told her they were finally on the right track. She had at least one huge hurdle to overcome, though. She was dead. She couldn't go to a judge and request a search warrant. She couldn't even make an arrest. And she wasn't willing to turn the case over to someone else.

"We've got more," Cots said, coming into the living room where Leah had retreated.

"What?" Leah asked.

"According to the maintenance department's records, Martin didn't use a chipper on the day of the murders. However, he was scheduled to drive one the next day to Central Park where a huge old tree had been blown down. Maintenance department records indicate that because it was New Year's weekend, he checked it out at the end of the day on Friday so he could get an early start Monday morning. Apparently, he often checked the machine out the night before a big job with the sanction of the department."

"Show me your surveillance tapes of his street," Leah said.

"Come with me," he said as he headed for the secure room.

Cots quickly had the tapes on the big screen on the wall.

"What are you looking for?" he asked.

"I have a dim memory of some sort of big maintenance truck parked on his street yesterday. I remember being surprised it was there."

Cots sped the tape forward to the Martins' street. Sure enough, there was a large truck in front of the house a few doors up the street from the Martin house.

"There it is," Leah said.

"Yeah, I remember seeing it, too," Cots said. "I think I can get a license plate number. I'll run it and find out who it belongs to."

"Good. Also find out if Martin was supposed to be working while he was home drinking beer and abusing his wife."

Leah returned to the living room and began updating the murder board. She was getting excited about the prospect of making an arrest in this case, somehow. First, though, she had to overcome some hurdles. Maybe her meeting with the commissioner would lower a couple of those hurdles. *At least I won't have to stay dead that way.*

"I ran the license plate from the truck," Cots said as he entered the living room. "It belongs to the city's maintenance department. It's checked out to Martin for a job he was supposedly doing yesterday."

"So he was supposed to be working when, in reality, he was home?"

"Yes."

"Good. It might be some leverage we can use against him in time."

"How so?" Cots asked.

"If he's been working for the city for nineteen years, he must be getting close to retirement. He won't want to lose his pension. If we hit him with the fact we can prove he's been at home while he was supposed to be on the job, he might be more willing to be helpful."

"Let's hope we won't need leverage because that sounds awfully lame to me," Cots told her.

"Yeah, I know, but right now I want to have as much ammunition as we can muster before confronting any of the players in this drama," Leah said, knowing she needed more evidence, but she also knew they were finally on the right track.

She made a list on the murder board of the things she'd need until an arrest was made. She'd need a search warrant in order to give Scotty access to the chipper. She'd need an arrest warrant to be able to take Martin into custody. She'd need to take Martin somewhere since her precinct was no longer in existence. Equally important to those things was finding out why the bishop had been killed. The wrong place, wrong time theory for his death felt right, but someone had lured him to the park, and that someone was as responsible for his death as the person who fed him into the chipper.

When she ran out of things to put on the murder board, her mind returned to her job. She knew she'd have to resign from the police force. She was strangely okay with that. She'd been a cop for twenty years. Maybe she'd take a real vacation, like leave the planet and go somewhere else for a while. She and Quinn had talked about that a few years earlier but hadn't actually done it. *What am I going to do about all these feelings I still have for Quinn? I can't be with her because I can't, won't, trust her again. But she still makes my heart beat faster when I think of her. How am supposed to stop my body and mind from wanting her?*

CHAPTER FOURTEEN

The next morning at eight thirty, Leah told Cots and Peony it was time to get on the road for their meeting with the commissioner. It took them fifteen minutes to get their winter gear on and get out of the condo; they were all ready to get away from the walls of the condo. Cots had them parked near the teahouse the commissioner had chosen for their ten thirty meeting by nine forty-five.

"Sing out if you see anyone you recognize," Leah said.

Peony and Cots had their eyes glued to the surveillance feeds on their computers.

"The guy standing at the corner having a smoke is a cop," Peony said.

"How do you know him?" Leah asked.

"He was in my class at the academy."

It only took them a few minutes to identify several cops near the teahouse. It didn't surprise Leah that Commissioner Robinson would travel with a large contingency of bodyguards considering the bombings, but this seemed a little excessive.

"Ready?" Leah asked Peony.

"Yeah."

"Let's go," Leah said, getting out of the van on the sidewalk side.

Peony followed her.

Instead of heading across the street to the teahouse, though,

Leah rapidly walked into the store nearest the van. If Peony was surprised, she didn't seem to hesitate. Leah was sure anyone watching them exit the van wouldn't be able to identify either of them because only their eyes were showing. The rest of their features were obscured by scarves and hoods.

Inside the store, Leah flashed her badge and said, "Back door?"

The startled clerk pointed toward the back of the store. Leah and Peony hurried through the nearly empty store and out into the delivery alley. Instead of turning toward the teahouse, Leah again led them away from their destination. Two blocks away, they crossed a busy street and entered a small neighborhood park.

When Leah was certain no one was following them, she turned toward the teahouse but continued to take a circuitous route to get them there. They exited the park and entered a nearby alley, leading them to the back door of the teahouse. They surprised the chef and his cooks as they walked through the kitchen and into the restaurant. When she flashed her badge, no one obstructed their entering the restaurant.

They sat at a small table where they had a view of the front door and the large window facing the street, and easy access to the back door. Leah was in no mood to trust anyone these days.

At precisely ten thirty, two men entered the teahouse looking distinctly out of place and uncomfortable. They were followed by Commissioner Shelley Robinson, who had two more men follow her. She chose to sit at a table away from the big front window.

Leah had met Robinson on a couple of occasions, mostly in the line of duty, at funerals and the like. Now she watched the woman take off her winter coat. Her eyes never stayed still. She was much more alert to her surroundings than the men guarding her.

Robinson settled in and gave her order to the waiter when the young man approached her table. The men with her returned to the main room after checking out the kitchen and bathrooms, and then, after a word from the commissioner, three of them stationed themselves outside the front door. Leah presumed there were a like number of men in the alley.

"Stay here." Leah put her credits card on the table. "Order something to eat and drink for yourself."

Leah left her coat at the table with Peony and went into the women's room. When she emerged, she went toward the commissioner's table. One of the guards stepped in front of her. She showed him her badge and said, "I'm Samuels." The guard stepped aside and she took the vacant seat, putting her back to the wall.

"Commissioner Robinson?" Leah asked.

She nodded.

"I'm Leah Samuels. You were expecting me, I believe."

"You're good. My boys should have known a cop of your abilities wouldn't stroll in through the front door."

"Yeah. Your guards need to anticipate your enemies."

"I'll keep that in mind. I don't suppose you'd like to head up my detail, would you?" Robinson asked with a smile.

"No, thanks."

"I didn't really think you would, but I had to ask. What can I do for you today?"

"I was assigned to solve the murders at Taconic Park."

"That's where Bishop Cohane was murdered, right?"

"Right."

How in the world does Robinson know about the bishop? Quinn probably told her. The media doesn't even know the bishop is missing. If Robinson tells the press, there will be a field day and my suspects could flee the planet. Phuc!

"Why didn't you check in to say you weren't dead?"

"I was already investigating my case and had moved off-site to keep the details of the bishop's involvement quiet. After the bombings, it made sense to stay put." The reason Leah had been trying to put into words for days came to her easily now. She wasn't about to bring up the possibility of the bombings being connected to her case, since she didn't have any evidence that was true. *Yet.*

Robinson considered that, her eyes shrewd. "I feel like there's more to this than you're telling me. And I don't guess you've made much progress in the case. I'm in the process of creating a task force to solve the murders since I didn't know someone was already working the case. Maybe you can give my team information."

"There's no need for that. I think I've found our killers."

"Great work, Lieutenant. You are as good as they say. Who are the killers you're looking at? What do you need from me?"

Leah thought Robinson sounded more disappointed than relieved.

"I need you to give me special powers," she said even as she ignored her question about the identity of the killers. It was her case, and it was her right to make the arrest. She wasn't about to have that taken away from her after all the work they'd done.

"Like what?" Robinson asked, obviously on the alert for some sort of trickery.

"I need a search warrant and an arrest warrant, so I need a letter from you telling a judge I'm authorized to investigate this case."

"Why do you need a letter? Isn't there a procedure in place for you to obtain your warrant?"

"There is. I would suspect, however, that a judge might be reluctant to issue them based on the word of a dead cop."

"Why don't I hold a press conference and tell the world that you've been undercover and are close to making an arrest? That would be good for your career."

"I'd prefer that you not do that until it's true," Leah said. "If you do that, my suspects could run, and then we'd never solve the case."

"I thought you said you needed a search warrant and an arrest warrant," Robinson said.

"I do. What if the evidence I get from the search warrant doesn't amount to enough to arrest my suspect?"

"I see," Robinson said.

Leah wasn't convinced she did see the implications, but she waited patiently and silently. She wasn't going to beg to be able to do her job.

"I'll get you the letter. Where shall I send it?" Robinson asked when it was clear Leah wasn't going to say anything further.

She pulled a fountain pen from her pocket. She took her time unscrewing the cap.

Drude, the woman is showing off her pen. Like I give a shit she writes with an antique fountain pen. Leah glanced around, but no one but Peony was watching them, not even her guards. So all this posturing was for her benefit. She debated whether to tell Robinson she thought old-fashioned pen and ink were affectations and the people who used them were idiots. Except herself, of course. She didn't say anything out loud. She wanted her warrants more than she wanted to tell her off.

"Send it to Quinn's office." Leah hated having to use Quinn, but there was no place else she could think of to have the letter sent to that wouldn't unduly expose the team. Leah wasn't about to give her address to this preening little peahen.

"I'll have it delivered once I get back to my office."

"Thanks," Leah said as she stood up.

"My pleasure. Be sure to let me know how it works out, and if you need anything, call."

Robinson stood up as well. She held out her hand and Leah reluctantly shook it. As she suspected it might be, Robinson's hand was damp with sweat and her handshake limp as an eel.

Leah returned to the table she'd shared with Peony and sat down. She shook out the napkin at her place, dipped it in her water glass, and wiped her hands. She took the glass of tea sitting in front of Peony as if it were her own.

"I didn't order you anything, Boss. I'm sorry. If I had known—" Peony looked embarrassed.

Leah interrupted her. "It's okay. I want Robinson to leave first. I'm not hungry." She glanced at Robinson's boys, but no one was paying any attention to her and Peony.

"Oh, right," Peony said, chewing as fast as she could. She looked like she was starving with no hope of ever eating again even though she had a breakfast just two hours earlier that would have put a dinosaur to shame.

Robinson seemed like she was at a loss about what to do next. One of her guards approached her and nodded toward the door. Robinson glanced over at Leah. She'd bet a month's salary Robinson wanted to know if she'd noticed her indecision. She rose from her chair and Leah nodded at her to show she had noticed the faux pas. She turned away from Leah without acknowledging her and left the restaurant as she shrugged into her coat. Her guards trailed after her. Leah watched as a long black car pulled to the curb in front of the door and stopped in front of her. One of the guards opened the back door, and Robinson climbed in followed by one of the men who had remained inside the restaurant with her. When the door closed, the black car pulled away from the curb and into traffic.

I don't trust her. She's not a real cop's cop. Where do they find these people they put into the commissioner's office? Leah waited another five minutes before getting up from the table and putting on her winter gear. Peony followed suit. They left the restaurant the same way they had arrived. In the alley, she glanced around but didn't see anyone lurking in the doorways that lined the alley. She took Peony back through the park and then to the van.

Inside the van, Cots, in the driver's seat, was busy with his personal computer. Leah and Peony climbed into the warmth of the van and lowered the scarves covering their faces.

"That went well, didn't it?" Cots asked.

"It did," Leah responded.

"But?"

"How did she know about the bishop?"

"I wondered about that. When I called she didn't ask a single question," Cots said. "What else bothers you?"

"Do you think it strange the commissioner didn't want any details?"

"What do you mean?"

"When I asked for search and arrest warrants, she didn't want to know what I wanted to search. She didn't ask for any details; she asked who I wanted to arrest, but she didn't ask again when I didn't answer. It was almost like she already knew what I know."

"Is it really possible she already has the details of the case? Wouldn't it mean someone told her? Are you thinking it was Quinn?" Peony asked, her eyes wide.

"Yeah, I am. Cots, call Quinn and tell her the commissioner will be delivering a letter for me to her office. And that you'll pick it up personally."

"You're not happy about having her involved again, are you?"

"No, I'm not, but I couldn't think of anywhere to send the letter. I couldn't give her the condo's address, so it was Quinn's office or go hang out in her office until the letter is ready. Quinn seemed like the lesser of the two evils."

Cots keyed on his phone and speed-dialed Quinn's number. Leah tuned out his conversation with her. When he hung up, Cots said, "She'll hang around her office until the letter arrives."

"We'll get it later. Thanks for making the call."

"Where to now?" Cots asked.

"Take us to the bishop's mansion," Leah told him.

When they pulled out into traffic, Cots said, "We've got company."

"Cops?"

"Yeah," Peony replied. "Wait, another car has joined us. And another. It looks like we've got ourselves a freakin' parade."

Cots guffawed while Leah grinned.

"You know what to do, Cots. My meeting is at two. Just make sure we're on time."

Leah sat back and enjoyed the game of cat and mouse they were playing with whoever was following them. Cots was good, though, and in the end, it appeared they had lost all the cars trailing them.

"Boss, listen to this," Peony said. She turned up the computer so they could all hear.

"At an impromptu press conference held only minutes ago, Police Commissioner Shelley Robinson announced one of the city's most highly decorated cops has been doing undercover work for her office. She declined to say who the cop is, what case he or she has been working on, or even why she was telling the media about it now without giving any details," a news reporter said.

"Drude!" Leah exclaimed. "What does the bitch think she's doing?"

"Did I hear wrong or did you tell the woman *not* to do a press conference?" Cots asked.

"You heard right. She's sabotaging the investigation."

"But why?" Peony asked.

"She's always been a bit of a media queen, don't you think? She's merely acting true to form and didn't give you a thought," Cots said. "But the fact that she didn't give any details of the case is a good thing, right? Sounds like she's just showing you who's boss."

"You're right. Thanks for keeping my paranoia in check," Leah said with a smile.

Cots flipped on his blinker and turned right. "Let's stop by Quinn's office and get Robinson's letter in case this meeting adds something more to your case. It's on our way to the bishop's office."

"Good idea." Leah wanted the extra time to think.

When Cots parked the van near Quinn's office building, he

got out and hurried across the busy street, deftly dodging the heavy traffic.

Leah sat staring out the front window not seeing anything. She wanted more than anything to believe that all this was only part of a bad dream, and she'd wake up from the nightmare to have Quinn safely ensconced in her bed and none of this shit would be true. Instead, she was getting close to finding out who was responsible for a mass murder, but in the process, she'd lost her wife, her career, and her faith in the job. She closed her eyes and slumped in her seat. *It's been a hell of a week.*

CHAPTER FIFTEEN

Thirty minutes after Cots left them, he returned.

"Sorry it took so long. Quinn wanted to talk. Here are your documents."

Leah glanced at them and noticed the print at the bottom of the page said they had been received twenty-five minutes earlier, which meant the commissioner must have written it the moment she left the café. She returned her attention to the document in her hand. As she read, she saw one of the documents wasn't what she had asked for. She had asked for a letter saying she was authorized to investigate the murders in the park and to get a search warrant. What she had in hand was a search warrant and two arrest warrants. She needed only to fill in the blanks about what she wanted to search and who she wanted to arrest. She looked at the signature line. It was signed by the commissioner, not a judge. *Does the commissioner of police really believe she has the authority to issue search and arrest warrants?* That made the warrants virtually useless. She could take them to the judge instead of a letter, as proof she was allowed to investigate, but she'd still have to find a judge to give her the real thing. *Does she think I'm an idiot?*

"Does anyone recall me telling the commissioner I wanted to arrest two people?"

Only silence answered her.

Drude. The commissioner obviously thinks two people are involved in the murders. But I've only got one suspect. Who does the commissioner, or her informant, think is the second person? Who gave her a second name? And why didn't she share that name with me at the restaurant? Someone was a step ahead of her, and she hated being in the dark.

Leah had them on the road and heading toward the bishop's mansion almost before Cots had his seat restraints on. She felt a sudden sense of urgency. If someone else had information she didn't, she needed to work faster to get to the end result before they did. "Who are we meeting with?" Leah asked, glancing over at Cots.

"A priest by the name of Joseph Preata."

"A man?" Leah asked.

She had been thinking, for some reason, the bishop's assistant was a woman. When she said it out loud, she realized how sexist she was being. *Where did that come from?*

"Yeah, a man. You didn't think the bishop would have a female assistant, did you?" Cots asked with a smile.

"No, of course not." Leah looked away. "Peony, find out what you can on Joseph Preata."

Five minutes later, Peony said, "He's clean as a whistle, Boss. He entered the seminary when he was twenty-two and has worked his way up the ladder to his current position over the last fifteen years. He's been appointed to a position at the Vatican and is due to assume his duties there next month."

"Thanks."

They rode the rest of the way to the bishop's mansion in silence. When they arrived, they sat looking at the impressive building set off the road and surrounded by a high fence. Unlike its neighbors, which were made of brick, the bishop's mansion looked like it could have been lifted from Tuscany and set down in this neighborhood. Its walls were the rich color of the soil she'd seen when she'd visited Italy with her aunt. There was a guard stationed at the front gate. She wondered why someone thought the bishop needed the protection of a guard—not that a guard at the gate would provide much protection, but still.

"Peony, you're with me."

After being admitted through the front gate, Leah and Peony were met at the front door by a priest.

"Follow me, please." He led them to an office near the back of the mansion.

As they followed the priest down the long hallway, Leah and Peony removed their hoods and lowered their scarves from their faces. A caress of heat hit her, and Leah nearly sighed out loud at how good it felt.

Leah was surprised when it seemed every room they passed was an office. She had thought the bishop's mansion would be more home than office, but she was mistaken. Maybe his living quarters were on the second floor. Or maybe this was strictly for business and his home was somewhere else. If the latter was true, she wondered how they'd gotten around the zoning laws for this neighborhood.

Focus. Stop wandering off on tangents. The zoning of this neighborhood has nothing to do with the bishop's death. Focus on the case.

At a door at the end of the hallway, the priest escorting them knocked twice. A voice inside the room called, "Enter." The priest escorting them nodded politely at them, turned, and headed back toward the front of the mansion.

Leah opened the door and they entered the office.

"Hello, I'm Joseph Preata, special assistant to Bishop Cohane."

Joseph Preata was movie star handsome. His black hair was graying slightly at the temples, and he looked like he was a swimmer, with wide shoulders and a trim waist. His eyes were the blue of a summer sky. He was taller than Leah by about three inches, and that would put him right at six feet tall.

"I'm Lieutenant Leah Samuels and this is Detective Peony Fong."

Leah had to lightly jab Peony in the ribs to get her out of her reverie about the priest.

"What a beautiful name," Preata told Peony with a smile, showing off his dimples. "You're undoubtedly from Xing."

"Yes, I am," Peony responded almost breathlessly.

He turned back to Leah. "Lieutenant, your reputation precedes you. However, didn't I read somewhere you were dead? Killed in one of the explosions that wiped out a police precinct, wasn't it?"

Leah was tempted to say something about having risen from the dead, but thought better of it considering who she was talking to. She didn't want to offend him because she wanted information, and it would be unlikely he would be cooperative if she pissed him off.

"The rumors of my death were greatly exaggerated," she said instead.

"I'm glad to hear it. How can I help you today?"

"I need to know the bishop's itinerary for the evening he went missing."

"I wondered about that myself after he disappeared. I checked both the calendar I kept for him as well as his personal calendar, and he had nothing scheduled. The only thing I can think is he got a call that was so urgent he went out into the middle of the blizzard. I wanted to retrace his steps to see if his car was lying in a ditch somewhere but had no idea where to begin to look for him."

"Did he do that often?"

"Go out in the middle of a blizzard at midnight? Or end up on the side of the road?" Preata asked with a trace of superiority on his face.

"In the middle of a blizzard."

"As far as I knew, he'd never done that before, at least not while he's been bishop here. But then, this is the first time he's gone missing for this long. There have been times he'd be missing for a few hours at most, but he always turned up saying he'd gotten lost and wandered around until he found something or somewhere that looked familiar. That's why we got him a driver."

"Where was the driver that night?" Leah asked, trying to figure out how the bishop had gotten to the field.

"He was told to take the bishop home and then go home himself because of the storm coming to town," Preata said.

"But?" Leah asked.

"But according to the driver, the bishop was insistent he be left at the cathedral. He told the driver he'd take a cab home." Preata tilted his head slightly. "And when the bishop insists, one does as one is asked."

"What's at the cathedral?"

"In addition to his offices here at the mansion, he keeps a small office at the cathedral."

"The driver was okay with leaving the bishop at the cathedral when a blizzard was coming in?" Leah asked.

"Not really, but the bishop could be very, shall we say, adamant. The driver knew the bishop would be safe in the cathedral and could sleep on the couch in his office, as he had upon occasion."

"Is there anything else you can tell me about that evening?"

"I'd like to believe he told me everything, but that would be naïve," Preata said. "There are always things that are on a need-to-know basis."

"Do you know if he had any dealings, either professionally or personally, with witches?"

Obviously, the question surprised Preata because his perfect eyebrows shot up practically to his hairline.

"I don't know of any dealings he had with witches. Although I do know he was opposed to the resurgence of the establishment of the local covens."

"How do you know that?"

"Twice a year, the religious leaders throughout the world come together to discuss the state of religion in this country and the nearby occupied planets. One of the topics under discussion at the last meeting was the number of covens springing up. The bishop said, at the meeting, he was adamantly opposed to them."

"When was the meeting?"

"I don't know the exact date without looking at my calendar, but I believe it was about six months ago."

"Were all the religious leaders opposed?" Leah asked.

"Not all, but certainly the majority of them," Preata said.

"Why? Did the witches pose some sort of threat to the bishop or to religion in general?"

"Not to the bishop himself, but to the Church. We believe you should only worship God. Witches worship the devil," Preata said.

"That's not true," Peony blurted out, surprising both Leah and Preata.

"What?" Preata asked. "That witches worship the devil?"

Leah didn't want to go off on a tangent. She gave Peony a look that told the detective not to go there.

"Did the bishop have any enemies?" she asked.

"He was beloved by all," Preata said. "No death threats, no hate mail."

Before Leah could ask another question, Preata asked, "Are you close to finding the bishop?"

"As a matter of fact, I am." Leah watched closely to gauge his reaction.

Preata didn't seem pleased with the news but seemed equally unsure what to say next.

"I understand you're being sent to the Vatican," Leah said, changing tactics.

"That's right," Preata said, and just barely kept his dislike of either the assignment or the Vatican out of his eyes, but not before Leah had seen the slight narrowing and a hardness appear that hadn't been there before.

"Is that something you wanted?"

"It is an honor to serve in the Vatican."

She smiled. "Yes, but did you want the honor?"

"I go where I can best serve God and the Church."

Leah knew Preata wasn't answering her question but also knew it didn't matter. She had picked up on the fact that while he gave voice to the party line, he wasn't pleased with being sent away.

"I know you've been a priest for fifteen years, and if the bishop is dead, would you be considered to take over his position?"

"I believe I would."

"So you stand to gain from his death." Again, Leah paid close attention to his expression, but he seemed to have gotten himself under control and didn't give anything away.

"Why, yes, I guess I do," Preata said as if it only then occurred to him he would be gaining a great deal by the death of the bishop.

"When will you know whether you'll be going to the Vatican or becoming a bishop?"

"When the Vatican announces it."

Leah knew she wasn't going to get anything helpful, so she stood up. "Thank you for your time," Leah said.

"You're welcome. If I can answer any other questions, please let me know. I hope you find the bishop very soon, and he's healthy and well."

The priest dismissed them at the door to the bishop's office that he obviously now thought of as his own.

As she and Peony neared the front door, Leah veered into the first office where there was an occupant. It was a young man, who couldn't be a day over twenty, with sandy hair, gentle brown eyes, and a desk covered with papers. He wore the traditional cassock. Leah idly wondered if cassocks were making a comeback.

Leah showed him her badge.

"Can I ask you a few questions?"

"Were you talking to Father Preata?"

"Yes, I was."

"Then I guess it's okay for me to talk to you as well."

"Did the bishop and Father Preata get along?"

"At first they did. But in the last few months, not so much."

"Why was that?"

"The bishop asked that Father Preata be transferred."

"Do you know why?"

The young priest looked around to make sure they weren't being overheard. Leah noticed Peony had stationed herself at the door to see if Preata was headed their way. *Well done.*

When he was satisfied no one was listening to their conversation, the priest said, almost whispering, "The bishop thought the Father needed to learn humility and thought the Vatican would be the place for that."

"What was the Father's reaction to being transferred?"

"He was angry. I think he had ambitions to replace the bishop when he retired next year."

Peony cleared her throat to let Leah know someone, most likely Preata, was approaching.

"Well, thank you for the directions. I would have gotten so lost without your help," Leah said in a louder voice.

At first, the priest was confused by the sudden change in the direction of their conversation. His face was flooded with relief when Preata stepped into the room.

"Still here?" Preata asked with a smile that didn't reach his eyes.

"I asked this young man for directions. I'm afraid I haven't spent much time in your area of the city and realized I had no idea how to return to police headquarters." Leah pulled the hood of her coat over her head.

"Ah. Well, have a safe trip," Preata said, obviously wanting them gone.

"Thank you," Leah said, her voice muffled by her scarf.

After passing through the gate leading to the street, Leah turned left and headed for the van.

"What did you think of Preata?" Leah asked.

"I've only met a couple of priests and they were kind, gentle men. This priest is anything but. I think he's arrogant and cold. He'd be hard to trust if he were my priest."

"Do you think he told us everything he knows about the bishop's disappearance?"

"I don't think so, but why would he hold something back? Does he not want us to find his boss?"

"Good questions. We need to find everything we can about him," Leah said. Something about the priest reminded her of a professional poker player—closed off, secretive, and wanting to win at all costs. "The question we need to answer is whether he's ambitious enough to set the bishop up to be murdered. What do you think?"

"I'm not sure he'd do the deed himself, but he wouldn't have any qualms about having someone else do it for him."

"Good. My thinking is he wouldn't be the trigger man unless the bishop made Preata angry, then he'd gladly pull the trigger. When we get back to the condo, find out if Frank Martin is a member of Preata's church."

The trip to the condo was without incident; no one tailed them, and the roads were cleared of most of the snow that had fallen the night before. Leah wondered if it was an omen that things might become clearer. *If only.*

When they were inside the condo, Leah went to the living room window and stared out her window. She started running over what they knew for sure. They knew... *Phuc.* They still didn't know anything for sure. They had a theory that the father of one of the victims in the field may have killed not only his daughter but twelve other young women because he hated his daughter and by extension the others in her coven. They didn't really know why or have any proof of that yet. They thought he might have used a wood chipper to what? Kill them? Or did he kill them some other way and then feed them to the chipper? God, she hoped the latter was true. *What else do we think we know?* The bishop was also a victim of the wood chipper–wielding madman. She needed just one hard piece of evidence. Maybe the search warrant would provide the piece of the puzzle that would allow them to put all the other pieces in place.

"It's a pretty day out there, isn't it?" Peony asked as she came to stand next to Leah in front of the living room window. "Too bad it's twenty below zero."

"It is a pretty day. It'll start to warm up in a few months." Leah hoped it was true and said it as much for herself as for Peony.

"To what? Zero?"

Leah laughed. "You'll be surprised how warm zero will feel after dealing with thirty below for several months."

Maybe I'll take a vacation after this is over to somewhere warm and just lie in the sun for a week or five. She wanted to let go of the fear and the worry about her case and her marriage, if only for a little while.

CHAPTER SIXTEEN

W hat did you find out about Frank Martin?" Leah asked an hour later when Peony returned to the living room.

"He and his family attend St. Martin's. It's Preata's assigned church. The Martins drive forty minutes in order to attend services there." Peony sipped a hot drink after she relayed her information.

"Probably because of the name connection," Leah said. "It would be something a man like Martin would do."

"Okay, so we have a disgruntled priest who believes he should be the next bishop of the New America Diocese, attending the same church as a bully named Frank Martin. What does it get us?" Peony asked.

"A step closer to solving this case," Leah said.

"How?"

"Assuming Martin is our killer, how would he get the bishop to an empty field in the middle of the night during a blizzard?"

"I doubt he could," Peony said.

"Me, too. So why would the bishop be there?"

"Because his personal assistant convinced him to be there or promised to meet him there?"

"Good. Now, what could the priest use to persuade the bishop to be there?"

"The coven," Peony said.

"And how would a priest know about the coven?"

"If someone who had knowledge of the coven told him."

"There you have it. One more nail in this case's coffin. I couldn't figure out those two things—how Martin could get the bishop there and how Preata knew about the coven—until we talked to Preata. Then it all fell into place. The fact the two men attend the same church was the clincher. Preata might have taken Martin's confession, and Martin mentioned the coven to his confessor. Maybe Martin told the priest his daughter was involved with witches. In any case, somehow, the priest used Martin to get rid of the bishop," Leah said.

"So the bishop wasn't simply in the wrong place at the wrong time. He was there because his assistant told him about the coven and undoubtedly suggested the bishop should put an end to it by showing up."

"I wonder if Preata thought the coven would kill the bishop. Or did he know what Martin planned to do and got the bishop there because of it?"

"Will we ever know the answer to that?" Peony asked.

Leah smiled wryly at the question. She could still remember that feeling of hopelessness on a difficult case when she'd been a newly minted detective. "Maybe not. Hopefully, though, one of them will give the other up and we'll get our answer then. First, though, we need to get a search warrant to see if Frank's chipper was used in these murders."

"I'll go back to seeing if I can dig anything up on Martin and Preata's connection," Peony said.

After Peony left the room, Leah called Scotty.

"Scotty, I need a machine processed as soon as you can do it," Leah said without any preliminaries.

"Good afternoon to you, too," Scotty said.

"Yeah, all that stuff," Leah said with a smile.

"How big a machine?"

"Do you know what a wood chipper is?"

"Isn't that what the parks people use to grind up tree limbs and trees?"

"That would be it," Leah said.

"You want me to process one of those things? They're huge."

"The one I'm interested in, Scotty, was probably used in the killing field murders. I need you to prove it."

He was silent for a moment. "Where in the world am I supposed to process it? Even the old lab couldn't have held that behemoth."

"While I'm getting the search warrant, why don't you figure it out, and let me know where to get it delivered" Leah asked.

"Uh, Leah?"

"Yeah?"

"Do we trust anyone yet?"

He sounded downbeat, and she wished she could help. "Not yet."

"So wherever I find to process this machine, it shouldn't be in one of the police labs, right?"

"That would be best. But we also need your findings to hold up in court. So wherever you go, make sure the evidence isn't tainted. I wanted this solidly tied up."

"Got it. I'll call when I've got a place."

"Thanks. Oh, and, Scotty? Any ideas on who we trust to serve a search warrant without alerting the world that's what we're doing?"

He was quiet for a moment. "Because you're supposed to be dead and dead people can't serve warrants. Got it. As far as I'm concerned, the biggest problem isn't serving the warrant but getting the chipper to my lab. I've got a guy on the transport team I think can keep his mouth closed. I'll give him a heads-up he may be needed once I find a space," Scotty said, sounding a little more positive. "He'd serve it for you."

"You're the best, Scotty."

"I know," he said and hung up.

Now she had to wait, and Leah hated waiting. At the same time, though, she knew she had to have patience. Normally, a member of her team would get the warrant issued by a judge while the rest of the team stood by at the place that was going to be searched, waiting for the warrant to arrive. Now, though, her team consisted of herself and Peony. And Cots, kind of. *I wonder if I could get a judge to issue the warrant electronically. Probably not.* A few years earlier, a judge had been badly burned when he issued the warrant not to the police but to the guy they wanted to arrest. The suspect had simply torn the search warrant up, packed his bags, got on his private jet, and flown off planet. As far as anyone knew, he'd never returned. The next thing the cops knew, the Judicial Council had issued new guidelines for warrants, and the only change was there were to be no electronically issued warrants and, therefore, no more egg on the faces of judges. She decided to concentrate on her murder board, and added her thoughts on the connection between Martin and Preata to the murder book.

Cots came into the living room as dusk began darkening the condo.

"I've got another connection for you. Three years ago, Mrs. Martin called the cops when her husband beat her up. She filed charges, but changed her mind when Martin agreed to get counseling. Instead of going to a shrink, he went to a priest."

"Let me guess. It was Preata?"

"It was."

"Do we know how long the counseling lasted?"

"Two weeks."

"That's all? That's not enough time for someone like Frank to get through the litany of violence in his family."

"Preata declared him counseled in a letter to the judge two weeks after accepting the assignment."

"Poor Mrs. Martin," Leah murmured.

"Yeah. The same day Preata issued his letter, Mrs. Martin ended up in the hospital. Multiple broken bones, contusions everywhere, and a busted spleen. She didn't press charges. In fact, she never even called the cops again, let alone filed charges against her husband."

"So we now know Preata knew Martin was a violent man. So when he wanted violence done, he knew who to turn to. Keep looking at Martin. The more we know, the more we have to help convict him."

Leah spent the rest of the evening waiting for Scotty's call and thinking. She ran the evidence they had over and over in her head looking for flaws in her thinking. She couldn't find any. She needed the physical evidence against Martin to be able to arrest him. Once she did that, she hoped he'd turn on Preata.

I will be so glad to put this case and all the other stuff intertwined with it to rest. Then I can begin to deal with my feelings for Quinn. Until then, I need to focus on the case. I don't want to make a mistake at this stage of the case because I wasn't focused. I can't deal with Quinn right now. The fact that she would have to deal with Quinn at all made her stomach churn. That was the last thing she'd ever have expected. Since that first bombing, her life had turned upside down, and it didn't look like it was about to turn right side up anytime soon.

CHAPTER SEVENTEEN

L eah had slept in the secure room, unable to bring herself to sleep in the same bed she'd shared with Quinn. As she lay awake in the early hours of the morning, she tried to get Quinn out of her mind. Every time Quinn popped up, she'd forcibly pushed her out of her head. "Focus" became her mantra.

When she finally gave up on going back to sleep, she showered in the guest bathroom and donned sweats, a sweatshirt that said "You Rule," and her favorite piggy fuzzy socks. She smiled when she looked down at her feet and saw the pigs flying. She went to the kitchen, made a pot of coffee, and sat sipping it while she waited for the others to join her. She ran over what needed to be done before she arrested Martin to see if she could find something to do with her day. There was nothing she could do until she heard from Scotty.

"Good morning," Peony said cheerfully as she and Cots entered the kitchen. Peony had given up any pretense of sleeping in her own room. Cots, always the grumpiest in the morning, grunted something that kind of sounded like "Morning," but could have been anything.

"Is it?" Leah hadn't even looked outside yet; the storm within her was taking all her attention and most of her energy.

"The sun is out for the second day in a row," Peony said.

"And there's an additional two feet of snow on the ground,"

Cots said sourly. As he was pouring his first mug of coffee of the day, he said, "Quinn called earlier."

He had his back to her, and Leah wasn't able to judge what he thought of the early morning call. He obviously wasn't going to volunteer what the call had been about.

She couldn't help herself as she asked, "Care to share?"

"She pumped me for information about the case. She specifically wanted to know who we were going to arrest."

"What did you tell her?"

"I told her we were going to arrest some guy who lived down in the tunnels," he said, referring to the miles of tunnels running under the city that a hundred years earlier had been used for transportation.

Peony started coughing, having guffawed just as she took her first sip of coffee.

"Quick thinking. At least if the commissioner announces that, we'll know who planted the story," Leah said, smiling.

Cots looked at Leah and returned her smile, but she saw the sadness in his eyes and knew it probably mirrored her own. He'd lost someone he'd known since childhood, and she'd lost a wife she'd thought she'd spend forever with. Now they were both operating on the assumption she was working against them. It sucked in ways she couldn't even express.

By midmorning, Leah was pacing the floor. She hadn't heard from Scotty, and she knew better from years of working with him than to call him to try to speed things along. With nothing better to do, she paced.

She glanced out the window and noticed Peony's sunny day had lasted all of two hours. Dark snow clouds were moving in rapidly from the northwest. For lack of anything better to do, she turned on a newscast to find out how much snow they could expect. Another twenty-two inches of snow was being predicted before this latest storm moved out of town. The good news was the temperatures were going to be slightly higher than the overnight temps. Leah smiled. The weatherwoman was obviously trying to be optimistic and cheerful. Leah wasn't sure how much difference three degrees would make when they were talking in terms of minus thirty-eight degrees.

"Leah?" Cots asked as he came in from the secure room.

"Yeah?" She turned away from the TV.

"Can we talk?"

"Of course. What's on your mind?"

"For what it's worth, Quinn doesn't represent all Devarians. She's always had the morals of a Forsythe toad."

"Thanks for telling me, Cots," Leah said. While she had no idea what a Forsythe toad was, she got the picture. "I have to admit, I'm still surprised you've taken my side over hers on this."

He shrugged. "Maybe it was a tipping point. Maybe it was getting to spend time with you and get to know you better. Maybe I just don't like being played. Whatever, I know I made the right choice." He looked at her speculatively. "Are you going to be okay?"

Leah had no idea what the answer to that was. "I think so. I mean, eventually, yeah. I don't feel like I knew her at all, and that makes me feel pretty stupid. I loved her, but I don't know if the woman I loved even existed. I want to ask her why she married me in the first place, but I'm not sure I actually want to know." She smiled at him sadly. "I hate not knowing what's going on, and I think that's pissing me off more than anything at the moment. What game is she playing?"

Cots shook his head and they sat silently for a long moment. Leah knew they were both out of words and unsure if there was anything more to say on the subject.

"Watch the news channel," Peony yelled from the secure room. She sounded almost panicky, and Cots grabbed the remote and turned to a news channel.

There was a picture of Quinn on the screen; Leah's heart began to race, and dread enveloped her.

"Another breaking story related to the disappearance of Bishop Cohane," a voice on the vidscreen was saying. "Quinn

Benubrian, the wealthy real estate mogul, has been murdered. Benubrian was returning to her office after a meeting and was gunned down as she exited her car in front of her office building. In recent weeks, rumors began circulating Benubrian was helping the police in the investigation of the Bishop Cohane disappearance. So far, there are no leads as to who was behind Benubrian's murder, and the police aren't saying anything more about the Cohane investigation." The vidscreen moved to a different scene. "And in another development, the Devarian Kings have been cleared of their involvement in the police station and crime lab complex bombings, leaving the rogue police detective as the only suspect."

Cots muted the vidscreen, his face pale and his eyes wide.

Leah sat down hard in a nearby chair.

Dead. Quinn is dead.

Someone killed her. Who wanted her dead? She couldn't believe what she was hearing. Cots, too, had found a seat on the closest chair, and Peony rushed in from the secure room to stand mute, having no words to speak.

Leah felt numb. Her mind was reeling and her thoughts were so jumbled they made no sense. *Dead. Quinn is dead. My wife is dead.*

A silence enveloped them, and no one spoke for several minutes. Peony cleared her throat and broke the silence.

"What is it?" Leah asked, glad for the distraction even as she felt her world spin further out of control.

"The newscast implied Quinn was, ah, killed because she was helping us investigate the disappearance of the bishop."

"Go on," Leah said.

"There are only a few people who knew Quinn was working with us on this case, at least at first."

"Grandini, the commissioner, and probably the governor." Cots counted them down on his fingers, and his hands were clearly shaking.

"Right. So of those three people, who would Quinn have the most dirt on?"

Cots scoffed. "Seriously? She could have files full of stuff on all of them."

Leah nodded. "True. So how does Quinn, and the information she was feeding people, tie them to the bishop case? Did she have information someone got particularly worried about?"

"Could it be Grandini who had her killed, and not because of any ties to the case?" Peony asked more to herself than to Leah and Cots. "More as a crime of passion kind of thing?"

Leah was glad Peony had asked the question she'd wanted to ask and wouldn't.

"Why would Grandini want to kill Quinn? She'd be more likely to kill Leah, don't you think?" Cots asked. "I think Leah's right. Quinn knew something too dangerous for someone to let her continue breathing."

Leah tried to quell the desire to vomit and turned her attention away from Quinn. "This is getting us nowhere fast. The commissioner will assign someone to investigate Quinn's killing, and I'm betting they find phuc-all. We need to stay focused on the killing field case. Cots, I understand the need for you to find her killers. I want to find them, too. But right now, I want to find out who killed the thirteen innocent young women in that field. I have a strong feeling that once we find the killer we've been looking for, we'll find the connections that lead us to Quinn's killer, too."

"Okay," Cots said reluctantly. "But we both know that because she's an alien, they won't spend much time on the investigation," Cots said bitterly.

"The good news is she's a wealthy alien," Leah said with a smile. "And they'll find out she and I were married, so that will help, too."

"How will they find out?"

"I'll tell them when the moment is right, although given the amount of information she passed on to people, I'm willing to bet plenty of people already know. So let's get our case resolved and see what they can do with theirs.

"One question is whether I come out of hiding so I can go to the morgue to identify Quinn's body." Leah couldn't believe the words were coming out of her mouth. The world felt surreal.

"You can't. Robinson didn't specifically identify you as the detective conducting the investigation of the Cohane murder. You've got to stay undercover until you make the arrests." Cots looked like he had the weight of the world on his shoulders. He was slumped in his seat, the perfect picture of dejection. "I'll do the identification."

Peony put her arm around him. "I agree, Boss. We've been effective in finding out who the killer is without the full weight of the department behind us. I think we should continue doing what we've been doing until we actually arrest the murderer."

Leah had been hoping they would say that. She wasn't sure yet how to deal with her feelings about Quinn and her betrayals. It felt like Quinn's death left her in kind of a limbo. She hadn't even really begun dealing with her cheating, and now she was dead. She felt, irrationally, that Quinn had cheated once more. Cheated her by dying and thus not allowing her to adequately process her emotions regarding what Quinn had done. Now she'd never get the answers to the questions she hadn't asked. *How can I rant and rave against a dead woman?* Leah mentally shook her head. *Focus!*

"Cots, what are we going to do about a funeral?" Leah asked.

"There'll be no funeral. I'll have her body shipped back to Devaria. She'll be cremated and her ashes scattered across our estate."

"But—" Leah started to say.

"Leah, she's not human. We don't bury our dead like you do. For generations, family members who die have had their ashes scattered on the estate. Quinn will be no different." Cots's tone was gentle but firm.

"Will you take her back?" Leah would respect their traditions. In their few years together, end-of-life matters hadn't come up, but what Cots said made sense.

"No. I have no desire to return home. The family will send someone to accompany the body to Devaria. I'll make the arrangements, but I won't go with her. Besides, I wouldn't be welcomed there."

"Why not?" Peony asked.

"When Quinn and I moved here, we underwent several operations to change our appearance so we'd be better able to fit in here. We didn't do that lightly since we knew we'd never be able to return to Devaria to live because we had become so…so human."

"What kind of changes?" Peony asked.

"Devarians, particularly upper-class Devarians, are…" Cots stopped as he presumably searched for the right words. "They, uh, look remarkably feline."

"Wow. Cool," Peony said.

"I've got digiprints of my family if you'd like to see them," Cots said more tentatively than Leah had ever heard him.

Leah was glad Peony thought Cots was once again "cool." Cots looked very relieved as well.

"You two go on. I'll look at the digiprints later," Leah said, not sure she could bear looking at Quinn as she'd been growing up.

Leah was beginning to understand she really had only superficially known her wife. She found it deeply disturbing she married a woman she knew so little about. She found she couldn't remember any deep, heart-to-heart conversations or even discussions about beliefs. She wondered what it said about her, about them as a couple. Also, she'd prided herself on being able to read people. How good was she at reading people if she hadn't been able to peg her own wife as being unfaithful and so blithely jeopardizing her career by passing information to the likes of Grandini? She forced her mind to turn away from the self-recriminations and move on to the relationship between Quinn and Cots. She'd assumed there was a close bond between the two, but now she wondered. But then, he was an alien, and he'd grieve his own way.

Leah's thoughts about Quinn were interrupted by her phone ringing.

"Lieutenant, Scotty here," the MSI said before Leah could say anything.

"What have you got for me?"

"A couple of things. First, I'm sorry for your loss."

"What do you mean?" Leah said warily.

"I know about you and Quinn. I'm sorry she's been killed."

"Thank you, Scotty. How did you know?"

"She was brought into the temporary morgue. I found a copy of your marriage certificate tucked into a fold in her wallet."

She carried our marriage certificate with her? Why would she do that? "What are you doing with it?"

"I checked the wallet into evidence, of course."

Leah wasn't sure whether the marriage certificate would go into evidence, too, or if Scotty would put it into his pocket. At this stage, she didn't care. It would have to come out she and Quinn were married sooner or later.

Scotty's voice returned her to the present.

"Before Quinn was killed, she told me about an old empty warehouse she owned. Perhaps I could use it to process the chipper. I went through it yesterday, and it would fit our needs perfectly. As her next of kin, you can give us permission to use it. I know it would mean coming out as her wife, but we need that space."

That was the question, wasn't it? How many times had Quinn gone behind her back, and who else had she told things she shouldn't have? "We're at an impasse in the investigation until you finish processing the chipper, so let's not stand on ceremony. I'll get the search warrant; you go to the warehouse and get it ready."

"I'm sorry for your loss, Leah," Scotty said. "If you need anything…"

Leah sat in her favorite chair in front of the living room windows after the phone call and speculated on why Quinn hadn't told her she'd told Scotty about the warehouse, and why she had. Quinn had to know she'd find out.

Leah wondered whether it would come out Quinn had been supplying the Grandini family with information on her investigations. She didn't know how long Quinn had been doing it, but she knew with a certainty born of instinct her investigation into the killing field murders had been compromised because of information Quinn had fed to Grandini, probably right from the beginning. The question was why. What was Grandini's interest in the Taconic murders? Quinn wouldn't have passed her information, and then kept pursuing that information even after Leah had told her to leave the condo, without reason. And who had Quinn given information to with regard to Leah's other cases over the years? Did the commissioner come into this? The governor? *Was I really just a pawn in some game I didn't know I was playing?* Quinn seemed to have information even after Leah had asked her to leave. She hadn't even thought to check and see if the condo was bugged, but that possibility made sense, given the amount of information people outside the condo were privy to.

She was brought back to the present by a snow removal truck making its way slowly down the street outside the condo. Its flashing lights seemed bright against the darkening sky. She turned the nearest vidscreen to a weather channel. The storm that had begun moving over the city earlier in the morning promised plummeting temperatures, which was just what the city needed—temps plummeting beyond endurance.

Later that night, after she changed the sheets for the third time since she'd asked Quinn to leave the condo, she knew it had started snowing again because of the deepening quiet that only came when a major snowstorm came to town. She lay awake listening to the quiet while trying unsuccessfully not to think of Quinn. She kept going over and over their time together. Had Quinn ever really loved her? Had Quinn married her because of what she was, rather than who she was? She wanted to talk to Cots about Quinn, she wanted to know more, but what if she found out things she didn't want to know? Suddenly, she sobbed heart-wrenching tears and couldn't seem to stop even to breathe. Her loss was not merely for Quinn, but for trust and love. Every fiber of her being wanted to believe Quinn had loved her, but everything she was finding out about her said she didn't. She felt the betrayal deep in her soul, and the fact that she couldn't tell Quinn, that she had to find a way to move forward knowing she'd never find closure, made the pain that much worse. What had been the truth, and what hadn't? All the lovemaking, all the hugs, caresses, and I love yous…were they just make-believe?

She finally fell into a troubled sleep with dreams full of Quinn being shot and dying alone on a city sidewalk. In her dream, she was there holding Quinn as she died and hearing her final words. Words said so low she couldn't quite make them out. When Quinn died, she howled to the sky one word, "betrayal." She awoke from her dream with her heart pounding an hour later and knew that while Quinn had betrayed her on so many levels, she had betrayed herself as well. At a gut level, she'd known Quinn hadn't been what she'd seemed to be. There had been other times, other questions left unanswered, that Leah had simply allowed to slide, afraid to rock the boat, afraid to get an honest answer. She'd stuck her head in the sand and gone forward with the relationship anyway, explaining away the lack of communication by using the fact that Quinn was Devarian. She wasn't sure who she was angrier with, Quinn or herself.

Leah heard a noise from inside the house. She lay still, trying to figure out what she'd heard. As quietly as possible, she pulled open the drawer in the nightstand next to the bed. She removed the weapon she kept there. She pulled her hand back beneath the covers because it was too cold to leave it outside the comforter.

She smiled when she heard the refrigerator door being pulled open. While she knew it was possible a killer or burglar would stop to help himself to a snack from the fridge because she'd seen such things occur on several of her cases, she doubted a killer would do so inside her house. She heard whispering but couldn't make out the words. She knew neither Cots nor Peony could sleep either. She wasn't the only one Quinn had left with questions, though she knew she was the one who'd been most betrayed.

My wife is dead, and I probably didn't really even know her.

She let the tears flow again until she fell asleep once more, alone and emotionally exhausted.

Chapter Eighteen

When Leah woke three hours later, she tried to remember her second dream, but it was already gone. She felt discombobulated and groggy. Her life stretched out before her, empty without Quinn. She felt a depression beginning to settle into her bones.

Forty-five minutes later, after a shower that helped wash away some of the evidence of her night spent crying, she joined the others in the kitchen. Cots looked like Leah felt, and Peony seemed to be at a loss. *Pull it together. Just get this case over with.* After sipping her first coffee of the day, Leah said, "We're going to get the search warrant signed by Judge Tarbor this morning. I've already called the judge's clerk and we have an appointment at nine thirty. We'll have to leave earlier than usual because of the storm, but I don't want to wait to get the warrant for the four or five days the weather people are predicting this storm will be stalled over us."

Although Scotty's guy was an option, Leah decided she wanted a backup plan, one that included people with badges. She called the new captain of the Thirty-fifth Precinct. She and Nikki Coleman had been friends since they were in grade school. Nikki had been one of the reasons Leah had entered the police academy. Nikki had gone through the academy two years earlier than Leah, and the stories she told about her life as a cop intrigued Leah. She, too, had wanted to catch bad guys.

"Nikki," Leah said when she answered her phone. "I need a favor."

"My God, you're alive," Nikki exclaimed. "Why does everyone think you're dead when you're not? Why didn't you come by the house? Are you okay?"

"That's a long story I will gladly tell you, but not right this minute," Leah said.

"You could have at least called to tell me you were alive." Nikki sounded hurt.

"It was better for you to not know. Things are pretty weird right now."

"I'll trust you on that for a little while, but not for long. What's the favor you need?"

"I need to borrow two or three of your most trusted detectives," Leah told her.

"Borrow?" Nikki asked.

"I need to serve a search warrant. There's only myself and one young detective working this case."

"Which case is it?"

"The killing field murders."

"Drude. I wondered who caught that case after you were killed. You're close to an arrest? You must be if you've got search warrants. Who are you arresting?"

An alarm went off in Leah's head. She was, she decided, getting permanently paranoid if she was suspicious of Nikki's questions.

"You know I can't tell you that, Nikki."

"I thought we were friends," Nikki said.

"So did I," Leah replied. "Can you help or not?"

"You know I will. I'll assign two of my best. Franklin and Taylor. Where shall I have them meet you?"

"I'll let them know. Give me their numbers. I have to get the warrant first."

"Which judge are you using?"

"Judge Tarbor."

"When are you seeing her?"

"Ten thirty. Why?"

"Just curious. I need to let Leigh and Taylor know when to expect your call."

After Nikki gave Leah the two detectives' phone numbers, they cut the connection. Leah sat wondering if she could really trust Nikki. The questions Nikki had asked weren't all that unreasonable under the circumstances, but still, they were somewhat unusual. She felt bad about lying to Nikki about when the judge was signing her search warrant, but she no longer knew who she could trust.

At seven fifteen, they began putting on their coats and getting ready to go see Judge Tarbor. After the van had warmed up, they headed toward the main courthouse.

Before getting out of the van, she said to Cots, "While we're gone, see what you can find on Captain Nikki Coleman and Judge Sandra Tarbor."

"Right."

At nine thirty, she and Peony were at the door to Judge Tarbor's chambers. The judge was waiting for them.

"Thank you for seeing us, Judge," Leah said. "This is Detective Peony Fong."

Judge Tarbor shook hands with them. "Lieutenant, I'm glad to see you've returned from the dead."

"Thank you. It's good to be back."

"You said you needed a search warrant."

"Yes, ma'am."

Leah handed the warrant provided by Commissioner Robinson to the judge and watched as the judge raised one eyebrow.

"This is already signed by the commissioner," the judge said, stating the obvious. "Although it oversteps her bounds somewhat, and I'm not sure it would stand up in court."

"Yes, ma'am. That's what I thought."

"So you specifically want my signature. That's fine. Why not go through regular channels?"

"The case I'm investigating may be somewhat iffy because chain of custody of some of the evidence due to the bombing of the Forty-fourth Precinct. I want all my t's crossed and my i's dotted. I don't want to jeopardize my case in any way."

The judge's eyes narrowed as she looked at Leah. "Why?"

"I'm not entirely sure that my two arrests won't, at some point, implicate several other people. When I make the first two arrests in this case, I'm thinking there'll be a lot of accusations flying about. Robinson's name might surface."

"Which case are we talking about?"

"The Taconic Park murders."

"The case involving the death of Bishop Cohane?"

Someone else who has heard that Cohane was found in that field. Great. Apparently, there was no secret about it now. "Yes, ma'am. It also may peripherally involve the murder of Quinn Benubrian."

"Who is your prime suspect in the bishop's murder?"

Leah knew she couldn't withhold information if she wanted help. "His personal assistant, Joseph Preata."

"What have you gotten yourself into, Lieutenant?"

"You haven't even heard the half of it, Judge."

"What you've told me is only half of it?" The judge looked incredulous but interested.

"The rest involves a city employee, a coven, and a wood chipper."

"Well, I can't wait to watch this one play out," the judge said, not unkindly.

"Actually, me, too," Leah said with a smile.

"You said the murder of Quinn Benubrian is part of your investigation?"

"It might be involved, but I'm letting whoever caught the case investigate her murder."

"Why?"

Because Quinn knew people she shouldn't have known. Because she had secrets. Because I refused to give up on this case and she's dead. "I have a personal connection with Benubrian."

"What's that?" the judge asked.

Leah wanted the search warrants more than she wanted to pretend she wasn't married to Quinn, and more than she was worried about it affecting her career. They were way past that now. "I was married to her," Leah said.

"This gets more and more complicated. And more and more interesting," the judge said.

"It does."

"I need to get to my courtroom. Good luck with the remainder of your investigation, Lieutenant," the judge said as she quickly signed the search warrant and handed it back to Leah.

"Thanks. Can I return for the arrest warrants?"

"Certainly. It won't hold much stock right now, but I can be trusted, and I'm on your side. Do what you need to do."

"Thank you." She was right, it didn't help much, but just hearing someone say they were behind her gave her a flicker of hope.

Leah and Peony walked through the courthouse that was now crowded with attorneys, cops, plaintiffs, and defendants. Before Leah could get back into her coat and scarf, she saw a couple of the waiting cops do double takes when they saw her, but she didn't stop and they didn't approach her. It was as if the cops weren't sure they'd seen what they'd seen.

In the van, she said, "Cots, do a quick search to see where the chipper is located."

A minute later, Cots said, "It's at the city parks and recreation's garage. It was taken out of service for repairs when Martin brought it back."

"That might be another name for destroying evidence. When did it go out of service?"

"At the end of the day yesterday," Cots said.

"Do you think someone alerted Preata or Martin?" Peony asked.

"It's possible, or maybe they're just being careful because they know we're looking around. Let's get a move on it and get to that garage, fast."

Cots broke a few traffic laws getting them to the city's maintenance yard. On the way, Leah called Taylor and Leigh, the two detectives from Nikki's squad, to have them meet her at the garage. She also let Scotty know where to meet them so he could be in charge of the piece of evidence right from the beginning.

When they entered the garage, Leah saw a chipper being raised on hydraulic lifts. She found the supervisor's office. The nameplate on the door said Don Sawyer.

Inside Sawyer's office, Leah showed her badge. "Stop work on that chipper now."

"You can't come in here and order me around," Sawyer said.

"Don't make me shoot you." Leah slammed her hands on the desk, making him jump.

"Which chipper are you talking about?" Sawyer was obviously stalling.

"The one on the lifts."

A quick look out the office window told both Leah and Sawyer that Peony had already stopped the mechanic from raising the truck too far off the ground. The mechanic was looking toward his supervisor's office, clearly waiting for orders.

As Leah and Sawyer headed toward the truck, Leah said, "Let me see the paperwork on that truck."

"I don't have it."

When they got to the truck, Peony handed Leah a greasy handheld computer. It was the work order.

"What are you supposed to do to this truck?" Leah asked the mechanic.

The mechanic, whose name tag said Brooks, looked to Sawyer.

"Answer the question," Leah ordered him.

"Martin said there's something wrong with the blades. They're not cutting the limbs anymore."

In one sentence, Brooks had confirmed what Leah wanted to know. The truck was Martin's.

"What would you do to fix it?"

"I'd have to take the whole mechanism apart to find out what the problem is. While I had it apart, I'd clean the blades and the housing. Then I'd have the blades sharpened. Then I'd put the whole thing back together again, good as new."

While he was at it, Leah thought to herself, the mechanic would destroy all their evidence. They had gotten to the truck just in time.

"We're impounding the truck," Leah said.

"You need a search warrant to do that," Sawyer said.

"Here you go," Leah said, handing the supervisor a copy of the search warrant.

Sawyer made a show of reading the warrant, as though that would change anything.

While Sawyer was doing that, Leah told Brooks, "Get this thing back on the ground."

Leah saw two men approaching them. They had to be Leigh and Taylor. They couldn't be anything but cops. Scotty came in behind them. "You Samuels?" the first cop asked her.

"Yeah."

"I'm Taylor and the kid is Leigh."

"Thanks for coming."

"Not much choice in the matter, but glad we can help out. What're we doing?"

"I've got a warrant to search this truck for evidence in a multiple murder case."

Leah knew it didn't take a particle physicist to figure out how the victims met their demise. She could see it only took Taylor a couple of seconds to get it figured out. Leigh was a few seconds slower and blanched when he realized what it meant.

"Where are we taking this thing?" Taylor asked.

"I've got a warehouse," Scotty said.

"How are we getting it there?" Taylor asked.

"I think Brooks here will volunteer to get it there for us, if we can find a way of getting him back."

"I think we can take care of that," Taylor said.

"Hey! Wait a second. Brooks has a job to do," Sawyer said.

"This thing is the job you assigned him to do today, so he'll still be doing his job when he helps us."

"He can't leave the premises."

"Don't make me shoot you," Taylor said, echoing Leah's earlier words.

"Fine. Take him. But don't be surprised if you find the mayor chewing on your ass," Sawyer told them as he turned away, clearly someone who watched too many crime shows.

"I'll ride with Brooks," Scotty told them eagerly.

"Scotty, the moment you find something…" Leah said.

Scotty didn't need Leah to finish that thought. He nodded and joined Brooks in the cab of the huge machine. He was grinning like a fool as Brooks moved them slowly out of the garage.

"What do you really need us for, Lieutenant, since you've already served the warrant and the evidence is being moved?" Taylor asked.

"I want to make sure Scotty is left alone to do his job."

"Ah. Protection service. What kind of case you got here?"

"Multiple murders. The suspect list is long and illustrious." Taylor nodded. "Are you willing?" Leah asked.

"You bet. Scotty's a good guy."

"That he is."

Leah and Peony returned to the van while Taylor and Leigh got in their car and followed the chipper out of the maintenance yard.

Cots was focused on his computer screen when Leah climbed into the passenger seat.

"Find anything?" Leah asked.

"Maybe. Probably. I'm following up on a few things," Cots said.

"In the meantime?" Leah asked.

"Your judge is clean. Not even a hint of impropriety anywhere in her background."

"I'm glad to hear that. I was hoping there was at least one decent judge left in the system. What about Nikki Coleman?"

"That's what I need to follow up on," Cots said, glancing at Leah.

"As soon as you can. Our list of people we can trust in law enforcement is too short as it is." *Please let Nikki be one of the good guys. I'm tired of questioning my gut.*

"Where to now?"

Before Leah could answer, her phone buzzed. "Yes?" she said.

"Leah, this is Shelley Robinson."

"Good morning, Commissioner," she said, wondering how Robinson had gotten her phone number. *Quinn probably gave it to her.*

"Good morning. I'm doing some follow-up on the case you've been working on." Even though she was technically her boss, she sounded tentative.

"Yes?"

"Are arrests imminent?"

"No, ma'am. We're still gathering evidence."

"Would you say you'll be making the arrests in the next week?"

"No, ma'am. I wouldn't say that."

"How about in two weeks?" Robinson asked.

"I think it's possible."

"Good. Let me know when you intend to make the arrests."

"Yes, ma'am," she said as she broke the connection.

"That was our esteemed commissioner wanting to know

exactly when we're going to make the arrests. I told her in two weeks."

"I thought we were going to do it today if Scotty can find something in the chipper," Peony said.

"We are. I don't want the commissioner making the announcement. If she does, Preata and Martin will disappear and we'll never be able to get them."

"You don't trust the commissioner, do you?" Peony asked.

"Not as far as I can throw her."

"How did she get your phone number?" Cots asked. "Only three people have the number: me, Scotty, and Quinn." Cots paused a moment and then said, "Never mind. Stupid question."

Cot's computer dinged at him. "Okay, found it," Cots said.

"Found what?" Leah asked.

"Nikki Coleman was accused of misconduct four years ago. She'd been promoted to captain a few months earlier. She was accused of, shall we say, creating evidence in a case against a suspected serial killer."

"I have a vague memory of that. She swore she hadn't done anything wrong."

"And she was right. She was proven innocent of all charges."

"What were you looking for?"

"I wanted to see who her accusers were and how she got exonerated."

"And?"

"Weston went to Internal Affairs and accused her of manufacturing evidence. Said he'd seen her do it. The hired killer worked for the Dragon's Eye gang and he was accused of killing sixteen people for the gang. Judge Tarbor was on the bench during the probable cause hearing. She bound the suspect over for trial after hearing the prosecution's case. He was eventually convicted and sentenced to death. Is this the Weston you fired?"

"One and the same," Leah said.

"He sure had a problem with women in power, didn't he?"

Peony asked. "How was Coleman cleared of manufacturing evidence?"

"All the evidence turned out to be rock solid, and the chain of custody preserved. There was no evidence any of it had been manufactured. IA gave her a clean bill of health," Cots said.

Leah's phone rang before they could discuss Weston's many problems. "Yes?"

"Leah, it's Scotty."

"Scotty, tell me it's good news."

"It is. I found blood and flesh on the chipper's blades. A quick DNA test showed the blood belonged to unknown females. I also found bone fragments beneath the blades. Best of all, I found a piece of skull, and it has a partial hole in it that I think we can prove is a bullet hole. I did a quick scan on hair left on the skull piece, and it belongs to the bishop. I think we've got enough for an arrest."

"You are, as always, Scotty, the very best."

"Thank you. Thank you. Go get 'em, Leah."

"I take it Scotty gave you what you needed?" Cots was already pulling onto the road.

"Yes. Take us back to the courthouse. I need Judge Tarbor to sign the arrest warrants."

When they got to the courthouse, Leah found the judge was still hearing a case. The judge's clerk sent a note into the courtroom saying Leah was waiting. While she waited, Leah paced the corridor outside the judge's chambers.

"That was fast work," Judge Tarbor said as she opened the door to her chambers.

"The crime lab supervisor is the best there is."

"He found something in the chipper?"

"Yes, there was blood and flesh on the blades."

"I do not like the image that conjures up."

"Then I'll stop there."

"It gets worse?"

"Yes, ma'am."

"Who are the arrest warrants for? I see Robinson signed blank warrants."

"Yes, ma'am. I was surprised but didn't point out her mistake. The warrants are for Joseph Preata and Frank Martin."

"I recognize the first name. Who is the second man?" Judge Tarbor read the arrest warrants as she talked.

"He's the one who fed the victims into the blades."

The judge signed the warrants and handed them back to Leah. "I hope you get your men, Lieutenant."

"Thank you, ma'am." Leah could feel the end of the case coming toward her and was glad it would soon be over even though she'd have to face her new reality. *Whatever that's going to be.*

On the way back to the van, Leah called Taylor. "Want to be in on the arrests?" she asked.

"You bet."

"Meet me at Forty-ninth and Broadway. I'll have the arrest warrant you'll need."

Forty-ninth Street was halfway between Martin's home and the bishop's mansion where Preata worked.

"There's a news flash you'll be interested in," Peony said from the backseat. She turned up the volume on the handheld vid screen.

"The Vatican," a reporter's voice intoned, "has announced that Joseph Preata has been appointed acting bishop of the New America Bishopric. As you may recall, Bishop Cohane disappeared three weeks ago. Until he is found, Preata will be acting as bishop."

"We're about to end one of the shortest reigns of a bishop," Cots said with glee.

Leah wasn't sure why Cots didn't like the Church or what he had against it, but he was clearly enjoying Preata's impending downfall. Maybe once this was over, she'd get to know Cots better. *Better than I knew Quinn.* She shook the thought off and forced herself to focus on the case.

Taylor and Franklin were waiting for them in a parking lot at the designated meeting place. Leah got out of the van and handed them the warrant for Preata's arrest.

"There's been a little complication. It was just on the news Preata's been appointed acting bishop. There's going to be a lot of media at his door."

"Lieutenant, are you sure you don't want to make the arrest, then? You've done all the work. You deserve all the credit."

"No. There are various reasons I can't, including the fact most people think I'm dead. You two go make the arrest. Take him to your precinct. We'll follow you with our guy."

"See you soon, then," Taylor said.

Back in the van, Leah said, "Take us to Martin's house."

She got her phone out of her pocket and dialed Nikki Coleman's number.

"Coleman."

"Nikki, I'm on my way to arrest one of the two men responsible for the killing field murders. Taylor and Leigh are arresting the other suspect. Can I use two of your interview rooms?"

"Of course. Anything else? Do I need to know anything?"

"I've sent Taylor to arrest Joseph Preata."

"The priest who was just appointed acting bishop?" Nikki asked.

"Yes. You okay with having him in your house?"

"Bring him on." Nikki laughed.

"See you soon," Leah said as she broke the connection.

When they got to Martin's house, his car was nowhere to be seen. Leah decided to wait for him to return and hoped he hadn't decided to take a vacation while his chipper was being refurbished. It occurred to her his supervisor might have called him to alert him she had impounded his chipper. She was betting on the fact the guys at the yard weren't any fonder of him than Mrs. Martin had been.

As they waited, Leah's phone rang.

"Yes."

"It's Taylor. The acting bishop isn't at his office or his home. His staff doesn't know where he is. What is it with disappearing bishops?"

"Stay put."

Leah's mind was reeling. Had someone alerted Preata and Martin she was coming after them and they'd managed to disappear? If so, who? No one knew they had the arrest warrants except Taylor and Leigh, and they hadn't known who was being arrested until fifteen minutes ago. *And the judge.* She hoped it wasn't the judge who had alerted the suspects. She liked the woman. Robinson had known enough to hand her two blank arrest warrants, which would indicate she knew she would be arresting two people, but did she know *which* two people she had in mind? It seemed likely, but was it probable? With this case, anything was possible, although with Quinn no longer supplying information, surely other people knew less now than they had. She decided she'd stay where she was for at least another hour in the hope Robinson hadn't known who she was after and Martin would return to his home.

Who else could have known Martin was a suspect? As she began mentally running down a list of people who might have known, a car turned onto Martin's street. There was a man behind the wheel.

As the car approached, Cots said, "It's Martin. Or at least, it's his car."

Martin pulled into the driveway. He got out of the driver's seat as the trunk lid popped open, and then retrieved three bags of groceries. After closing the lid with his elbow, he went to his front door, managed to get the knob turned without dropping any of his bags, and entered his house. He left the door open. Leah noted he hadn't bothered to lock his front door when he had left to go shopping.

"You stay here," Leah told Cots.

Leah and Peony got out of the car and went to the front door.

"Mr. Martin?" Leah called.

"Yeah, come on in," he yelled.

As Leah and Peony entered the living room, Martin came in from the kitchen.

"What do you want? I don't know where my wife is. The last time I saw her was when she was leaving with you."

"Frank Martin, I am placing you under arrest for the murder of Bishop Cohane, your daughter, and twelve others."

Leah quickly read him his rights. She left her weapon holstered but was ready to grab it, if necessary. She wanted information, and she wouldn't get it if he was dead.

"Do you understand your rights?" Leah asked.

"Yeah, yeah," Martin said.

Something's wrong here. He's too calm, too cocky. "Check the rest of the house," Leah told Peony.

Peony drew her weapon and headed for the back of the house and the bedrooms there.

Leah removed her restraints and approached Martin. She stopped just outside his reach.

"Put your hands on your head and turn around," Leah said.

Surprisingly, Martin did as he was told. Leah approached him cautiously. She grabbed his right arm at the wrist and pulled it down and behind him. She clipped the restraint onto his wrist. When she moved to take his left arm, he wheeled on her, almost knocking her down. She'd expected it, and he swung at her but only landed a glancing blow off her right cheekbone with the huge ring he wore on his left hand as she stepped backward. She noted the pain, but years of training came back to her. She punched him as hard as she could in the diaphragm, knocking the breath out of him. While he was trying to catch his breath, she drove her fist into his already-broken nose. He sank to his knees. Within seconds, she had him facedown on the floor and his left arm yanked up behind his back.

"Hey, you're hurting me!" His voice was muffled by the blood from his nose.

"Give me your arm," Leah growled at him, yanking harder on the right one.

He quickly put it behind him.

"Stop right there," said a voice from the doorway to the bedrooms.

Leah looked up after she finished cuffing Martin.

Preata had an arm around Peony's neck and a gun to her head. Fortunately, although she looked scared, Peony wasn't panicking.

"Don't do anything stupid, Preata." Leah looked for an opening, trying to figure out what her next move was.

"That's my line, Lieutenant." He smiled at her, but there was ice in his eyes.

"What do you want?"

"I'm going to walk out of here, and I'm going to take your detective with me. I want a jet waiting for me at Baseline Airport."

"I'm not going to let you walk away from a multiple murder charge." She planted herself between Preata and the door, her arms crossed. He'd have to get close to her to get her to move. Maybe that would be her chance.

"Then I'll kill your detective." He shrugged like it didn't matter to him.

"Whatever happened to 'Thou shalt not murder'?" Leah asked.

"That's as archaic as the rest of the dribble."

Leah was surprised. She wondered what possessed the man to go into the priesthood if he didn't believe its teachings. "Be that as it may, it's my job to arrest you for the murders of Bishop Cohane and thirteen others. How'd you get Martin to do your dirty work for you?" If she could keep him talking and waste time, Cots would figure out something had gone wrong. If he called for backup, everything would be okay. If he didn't, well then...

"It was too easy. I knew he hated the fact his daughter was a member of that stupid coven. I simply told him a few dozen times it was God's will and his duty as a father to make sure the coven and its members were eradicated. The idiot told me how, when, and where he was going to do God's will."

Leah was pleased Preata couldn't resist bragging. The longer she could keep him talking, the more likely it would be he would make a mistake and she could exploit it. "How'd you get the bishop to the field?"

"I drove him, of course."

"You drove him there yourself?"

"Yeah. I convinced him he should put a stop to devil worship and told him where the coven was meeting. He was stupid enough to think he could just show up and convert them."

Leah could see Preata's hand with the gun in it was getting tired. It was beginning to tremble, and the gun was no longer pointed at Peony's temple. Now, however, it was pointed at her throat.

Leah took a tiny step toward Preata, but he leveled the gun once more.

"I know what you're doing, Samuels. And it won't work. I'm already responsible for the killing of a bishop. It won't matter much to have the tag 'cop killer' added on. You won't walk out of here alive. Actually, I should kill Martin there, too. Make it look like Martin resisted arrest."

"Hey. You promised me I was doing God's work and I wouldn't go to jail," Martin said.

"Shut up, stupid."

"Don't call me stupid," Martin said as he started to roll over.

Leah put her foot on his back to keep him facedown. "Don't move."

"Yeah, lie there like the dog you are." Preata spat out a mirthless laugh.

Preata seemed to be trying to goad Martin into trying to get to his feet to give him the distraction he needed to kill all three of them. Leah kept her eyes on Preata and her boot planted firmly on Martin as Cots moved silently into the room behind Preata.

"I've always wanted to blow a priest to hell," Cots growled as he put his gun to Preata's head.

It was distraction enough for Peony to grab Preata's gun hand by the wrist and twist. Leah heard the bones breaking from across the room. The gun clattered to the floor. Peony kicked the gun away and quickly had the priest on his knees and restraints on him.

"I thought I told you to stay where you were," Leah said to Cots.

"I didn't want to miss the fun. I was watching from the van with my trusty binoculars," he said. "But I thought I'd let you chat awhile before coming to your rescue. You know, in case he said anything useful." He grinned at her.

Taylor and Leigh rushed into the room with weapons drawn. *Doesn't anyone do what I tell them anymore? I'm losing my touch.* Leah sighed, but relief flowed through her.

"Well, drude. We came to rescue you, Lieutenant. But it looks like that job's been done." Taylor put his gun away and smiled at her.

Rushing into the room behind them were two uniformed officers.

"Here's your backup," Taylor said with a grin.

Without anyone noticing but Leah, Cots stuck his gun into his pocket. He slipped out of the room the same way he'd come into it. Leah suspected since he hadn't trusted the city's boys in blue before he started working with Leah, he trusted them a whole lot less now. She let him go.

"How did you guys know what was going down here?" Leah asked.

"One of his neighbors called and told us," Taylor said.

Leah knew it hadn't been a neighbor making the call, it had been Cots. He had called Nikki and told her about Preata holding her and Peony at gunpoint before he'd come in himself.

"Your captain has two interview rooms waiting for us. Let's get these two into them as quickly as we can," Leah said.

"Quincy, take the fat guy on the floor with you. We'll take the priest with us," Taylor told one of the uniformed cops.

"Read him his rights on the way." Leah wasn't about to let a technicality get in the way of a conviction, and at this point, she'd simply have to trust she had good cops on her side.

After the others were gone, Leah called Nikki. "Thanks for sending Taylor and Leigh to our rescue." She was glad her paranoia hadn't messed up her friendship.

"I just got a call from Taylor, who said you already had both suspects in restraints."

"If you want to stay involved, you can have your team search the living quarters of Joseph Preata and the home of Frank Martin. You'll need search warrants, though. My search warrant only covered Martin's chipper."

"Of course I want to stay involved. Where are they now?"

"They're on their way to you as we speak."

"I hope you're right about all this, Leah. Arresting a priest is serious business in this town," Nikki told her. "Regardless, though, I'll send my teams out."

Leah laughed. "He did us a favor and bragged in true villain style. He admitted to all of it, in front of me and my detective. I'm not worried about being wrong." She hung up after saying she'd check in shortly.

"Are you okay?" Leah asked Peony.

"I think so. Is there any way we can keep it a secret I was bested by a priest?" Peony asked with a grin.

"I'll see what I can do, but I make no promises."

"Boss, you're bleeding pretty bad from the gash on your cheek. We need to get you to a hospital," Peony said.

"No hospital," Leah said. She hated hospitals. She'd spent way too much time in them as a rookie cop with a beat. There was too much pain and death in hospitals. She wanted nothing to do with them.

"At least let Cots clean you up and put a bandage on the cut so you look a little less like some sort of space pirate. That, or we can go to the hospital on the way back to the precinct to have it stitched up."

"Neither of those options are viable. Let's get to Nikki's house and wrap this thing up."

As they headed to the van and Cots, Leah was glad this case was finished. She would probably have to testify at Preata's and Martin's trials. After that, there was a good chance she'd no longer be a cop, and she wasn't sure that would be a bad thing. She simply didn't know whether she still wanted to be a cop. She knew she needed time to process Quinn and everything related to her, but she didn't even know how to begin to do that.

CHAPTER NINETEEN

"We're not going anywhere until you let me look at that wound," Cots said when they got back to the van.

"It's nothing. I'll take a shower when we get home," Leah said, waving him off.

"No, you'll let me look at it and clean it now or we're going to the hospital. Those are your choices here, Leah."

Leah sighed. Why did these two think they could order her about? *I'm not a fragile flower afraid of a little pain and blood.* She wouldn't go to a hospital so she let him clean the wound, but she wasn't happy about it.

"You need BodyBound or you'll have a scar," he told her.

"I'm not going to the hospital," she said emphatically. "Scars add character."

The only place to find BodyBound, though, was at the hospital. It hadn't yet been released for use by the general public. The doctors' lobbying groups made sure of that.

"Let me try something I read about a while ago. They're called butterfly stitches. You'll still have a scar, but it won't look as bad as if we do nothing now," Cots said.

"Where did you read about them?" Leah asked.

"What does it matter? You only have three choices. You can go to the hospital or you can have butterfly stitches."

"What's my third choice?" Leah asked.

"I have a needle and thread in my kit," Cots said.

Leah didn't see that she had three choices at all. The mere thought of needle and thread made her nauseous. Butterfly stitches it would be.

"How long will the stitches take?" Leah asked, capitulating without seeming to.

"About a minute and a half."

"Then do it."

Cots was right. It did take less than two minutes to apply the stitches. It didn't hurt as much as the cleaning had, and that was a good thing. After he finished, he sat back to admire his work.

"Don't do anything that puts a strain on those stitches. If any of them come loose, I'll drop you off at the hospital. Understand?" he asked sternly.

Leah gave a single nod of understanding. She wasn't sure what would dislodge a butterfly stitch, but she knew it wasn't anything she wanted to test.

Cots had just finished cleaning up his doctor stuff and putting it all in his kit when several squad cars pulled up to the Martin house.

Leah had a short conversation with the sergeant in charge, directing him to look for anything at all that connected the men, as well as anything else that seemed out of place. She could only hope at this point there weren't any cops who felt the need to hide evidence because of their personal beliefs. The case was no longer hers to keep to herself.

When she returned to the van, she told Cots to take them to Nikki's precinct house. As they neared the precinct, Cots said, "I need to do some grocery shopping. Call me when you need a ride home."

Leah laughed. His reluctance to be around cops mirrored her reluctance to be near a hospital. She sent him on his way.

When she and Peony walked into the squad room, it became deathly quiet. She hadn't expected a marching band, but this quiet was disconcerting.

"What's going on? Are we in trouble?" Peony whispered, concern lacing her voice.

Before Leah could answer, a buzz began. She knew they were talking about her and Peony, but she wasn't sure why.

Nikki motioned them into her office.

"You're quite the celebrities," she told them after Leah introduced her to Peony.

"Why?" Peony asked.

"Why? Let me count the ways. You captured the killers of fourteen people by yourselves, without help from the department. One of the men you arrested was a priest and the acting bishop, who apparently killed his predecessor. I say again, I only hope you know what you're doing, Leah. By the way, you look terrible." Nikki looked her over.

Leah glanced down and, for the first time, noticed the blood on the front of her blouse. She must have bled more than she'd realized.

"Did you go to the hospital or see a doctor?"

"Saw a doctor." She elbowed Peony when she was about to interject.

"He did a piss-poor job of fixing that gash," Nikki said. "I've got a clean blouse in my drawer. Why don't you put it on?"

From the tone of Nikki's voice, Leah knew it wasn't really a question. It was an order.

Nikki handed Leah the clean blouse, and she headed for the bathroom to change. Once there, she glanced in the mirror and immediately understood why Nikki had wanted her to change. She looked like she'd been hit with a plank of wood. She quickly stripped out of the bloodied blouse and stuffed it into the recycler and watched it disappear down the chute. Next, she took a handful of towelette packages and one by one opened them and cleaned the residual blood off her face, neck, and chest. After she put Nikki's blouse on, she at least looked somewhat presentable.

"Have you started interrogating them?" Leah asked Nikki when she returned to Nikki's office.

"No. It's your case."

"We got a confession from Preata at the scene, but we hadn't read him his rights yet."

"He gave you a spontaneous confession?" Nikki asked.

Leah glanced at Peony, who shrugged.

"He had a gun to Peony's head. I guess he thought it gave him the upper hand and he'd get away from us."

"That was pretty stupid of him, wasn't it?" Nikki asked.

"Yeah, it was," Leah said with a grin, which caused the wound on her cheek to ooze. She winced and went to wipe at it, but Nikki stopped her.

"Nasty cut there," Nikki said again, handing her a bandage and a roll of tape. "You really ought to go to the hospital and get BodyBonded."

"I've got stitches. That's all I'm going to do about it. Let's get this show on the road." Leah motioned toward the door.

"Who do you want to talk to first?"

"Preata. I want him to confirm what he told us at the house."

"He's in Interview One."

Leah and Peony left Nikki and went toward the interview room. There were even more people in the room than before, and several called out praise as they walked through. Leah simply nodded, and Peony looked bemused.

"Do you want to try your hand at Preata?" Leah asked when they got to the interview room.

"Really?" Peony asked.

"If you're up to it."

"The son of a Drularian she-dog had a gun to my head. Of course I'm up to it."

Leah smiled. "Let's go, then."

They neared the interview room, and Leah stopped. "Help me put this bandage on. I don't want to be distracted by blood oozing down by cheek."

Peony was quick and efficient and had the gauze bandage

over the wound in seconds. She taped it down and stood back. Leah was surprised at how efficient she was and how gentle.

"Thanks," Leah said. "Let's do this."

At the door to the interview room, Leah said, "Recording on. Lieutenant Leah Samuels and Detective Peony Fong conducting the interview of Joseph Preata, who has been read his rights and declined representation at this time."

When they entered the interview room, Leah knew both an oral and a visual recording of the interview were being done. She was surprised Preata didn't start screaming for an attorney right away. His injured wrist was resting in his lap, but he didn't complain about the pain or ask to see a doctor.

"Mr. Preata, my name is Lieutenant Samuels, and this is Detective Fong. First, I want to confirm Detective Taylor read you your rights. Is that correct?"

Preata nodded.

"Let the record reflect Mr. Preata has nodded."

Leah nodded to Peony to take over the interview.

"Can I get you something to drink?" Peony asked politely.

"I could use a cup of coffee," Preata said.

When the coffee was delivered moments later without Peony or Leah having left the room, Preata didn't question how someone had known to deliver the coffee to him.

"Mr. Preata, you stated you told Mr. Martin it was God's will he kill the members of the coven of witches and Bishop Cohane. Is that correct?" Peony asked, her voice a little shaky as the adrenaline caused by having a gun pointed at her head by the man sitting across from her began to dissipate.

"No, it is not. It's true I told him it was God's will he take his daughter out of the coven. When she refused to leave, I suggested he do something about it," Preata said, his eyes as cold as the Arctic in January.

"I see. Mr. Martin doesn't seem particularly bright. Did he get your meaning?"

"No, of course not. I had to explain it in detail to the cretin."
Preata's disdain for Martin was clear.

"That must have frustrated you."

"It was beneath me to have to deal with such stupidity, yes."

Leah wished the man would do something stupid himself so
she could hit him.

"What did you do?"

"The only thing you can do with people like him. I eventually
had to describe it to him in detail before he understood my
meaning."

"That must have been painful for you."

"You have no idea how painful. In the end, I had to tell him
the coven needed to die so there wouldn't be just one victim. He
hated women enough it wasn't hard to convince him it was God's
will."

"Did he believe you?"

"Of course he did. I'm a priest." Preata looked at Peony like
she was as stupid as Martin.

"How did he kill the women?" Peony asked.

Leah could see her knuckles were white where she had her
hands clasped in her lap, but her expression didn't show a thing.

"He put them into his chipper. I didn't see him do it, I just
saw him put the bodies in the truck." He rolled his eyes like they
were wasting his time.

"What truck?"

"He had a little truck attached to the back of the chipper. He
used that to move the bodies to the chipper."

"How in the world did you convince the bishop to go to the
field?" Peony asked, changing the subject.

"He wasn't any smarter than the cretin."

"What do you mean?"

"It was easy to convince him his presence at the coven's
meeting would turn those girls around and return them to the
bosom of Christ and the Church."

"Did you tell Martin to leave evidence of the bishop in the field?"

"Certainly not. Why would I do that? I was hoping he'd erase all evidence of the bishop's existence. I didn't want him ever to be found. If you found something to identify him by, it was Martin's stupidity rearing its ugly head one more time."

Peony worked him until they had all the details. Preata's eyes blazed with the fury of the zealot, and Leah wondered if being caught had snapped something in his brain.

"I was at the scene to make sure Martin didn't lose sight of what God and I wanted him to do. The bishop tried to stop him, but he was convinced he was doing God's work and the bishop was a devil in disguise. Still, he didn't want to kill the bishop. In the end, I had to do it myself. And there wasn't a cop in sight during the whole thing. Beautiful." Preata laughed.

"The whole thing?" Peony asked innocently.

"That's right." He leaned forward as though to confide in her. "Do you know how lucky we are to have so many cops willing to look the other way for a bit of money?" He laughed, his eyes unfocused. "Hell, when I found out a piece of the bishop was found, I even had one willing to blow up a bunch of other cops. He barely took a breath before he took the money I offered him, and that meant I didn't have to worry about the evidence anymore. 'Course, I asked another cop, too, as a backup, but she ended up backing out. Too bad she didn't die with the others."

Leah, who was standing in the corner behind Preata, nodded at Peony. Just like that, they had the connection Leah's instincts had said was there all along. Their job was almost done.

"Oh, one last question. Why did you kill Quinn Benubrian?" Peony asked, without looking at Leah.

Preata looked at Leah when he answered. "Stephan Grandini, the former head of the Grandini family, had been a long-time supporter of the Church and of my career in particular. When the Church and the people running the business side of the city work hand in hand, it's a big win-win. He'd done me a favor when I was younger. When one of Stephanie's people called Monday and said she needed a favor, I refused at first because it'd be too dangerous. I was told it was either Benubrian or me. Apparently, Benubrian stepped out of line, was refusing to play by the rules. She'd been supplying information to keep us all in the loop, but the little game they were playing with you backfired and you tossed her to the curb. That meant she wasn't valuable anymore. I mean, she still had her way of giving us something, but it wasn't enough. Plus, Stephanie's man said she knew about what had happened in the field. I couldn't figure out how he knew, but he had the details. So I could hardly refuse his request, could I?"

"What did he ask you to do?" Leah leaned against the wall, letting it hold her up, hoping she didn't look as shaky as she felt.

"Kill Quinn Benubrian. I already knew from killing the old man what it felt like to be God, so I had no qualms about doing it again. I approached Quinn on the street outside her office. It was easy. God was there in my hand when I pulled the trigger."

Leah indicated they needed to leave the room. She was close to pulling her weapon out and putting it to the priest's head. She wondered if they would ever find out why Grandini had really ordered the hit on Quinn. Peony, pausing long enough to take the cup Preata had drunk from, followed Leah out of the room. Scotty could use the cup to verify any of Preata's DNA he found on the chipper or, with luck, the weapon Preata held on Peony was the weapon used to kill the bishop and Quinn.

"What made you ask about Quinn?" Leah asked as they stood in the hallway.

"He was in a confessing mood. I thought maybe we'd get lucky and he'd know something about Quinn's murder," Peony said. "I didn't think for a minute he was directly involved. And for him to just come out with the info on the bombings…" She shook her head, looking truly baffled. "I mean, wow. The guy seems to have lost his mind."

"Good work, you two," Nikki told them as she came around the corner.

"You heard?" Leah asked.

"Yeah. Half the precinct's in the observation room. Come to my office."

"I'm going to go find something to eat," Peony said and walked off.

Leah waved and followed the captain back to her office.

"Tell me what's going on with you."

"What do you mean?"

"You've never been one to not take credit where credit's due."

"To be honest, I'm exhausted. This hasn't been the easiest case to deal with, and there's personal shit going down in the middle of it."

"You mean with your wife being killed by Grandini?"

"You know?" Leah was shocked to the bottom of her boots.

"My friend, almost everyone knows. And they respect you enough to keep your secrets secret."

Leah was close to tears at hearing Nikki's words.

"By the way, that's some detective you've got working for you. I thought you said she was a rookie. She conducted that interview like she'd been on the force for years," Nikki said.

"She's a natural. You should put in a request to have her reassigned to your house."

"I'll do that before someone else tries to snatch her up. How about you? Do you want to work here?"

"What I'd like to do is interview Martin, get some dinner, go home, take a shower, and go to bed," Leah said, evading the question. She had no idea where her path would lead once she left the building.

Nikki nodded, seeming to understand. "He's in Interview Two. And I know an evasion when I hear one."

Leah gave her a tired smile before leaving her office and

looking into the bullpen. "Peony." Leah saw her surrounded by a gaggle of detectives when she walked out of Nikki's office.

"Yes, ma'am?"

"We need to interview Martin before we can leave. Take the lead. You're good at this."

"Thanks," Peony said with a grin.

They headed to the interview room, and Leah was glad Peony was taking the lead. She was exhausted, physically and mentally, and she just wanted this to be over. Before entering the interview room, Leah said, "Recording on. Lieutenant Leah Samuels and Detective Peony Fong conducting the interview of Frank Martin, who has been read his rights and declined representation at this time."

"It's about fuckin' time you got here," Martin said belligerently as he stood up.

"Sit down," Leah said firmly.

When Martin remained standing, Leah took a step toward him. He quickly retook his seat.

"I'm Lieutenant Samuels and this is Detective Fong. We've got a few questions to ask you. Before you say anything, let me tell you Preata has told us that killing the girls and the bishop was all your idea." Leah hoped that by jumping to the meat of the matter, they'd forestall his request for an attorney.

She was rewarded when he said, "He's a lying sack of Drularian dog shit."

Peony sat in the chair across the table from Martin.

"What do you mean?" Peony asked.

For the next half hour, Martin implicated not only Preata but himself as well. Peony remained calm and exuded innocence and sweetness throughout the gruesome testimony. He confirmed Preata had killed the bishop when he said he couldn't do it because he was a "man of God."

"Mr. Martin, *how* did you kill those women?" Leah asked when Peony didn't.

"I told you. I put them into the chipper," he said wearily.

"They were still alive when you fed them into the chipper?"

"What do you think I am? Some kind of monster?" He looked at her incredulously.

Leah raised an eyebrow and returned the look. "Let's see. You killed thirteen young women and you wonder why we might think you're a monster?"

"I'm not a monster. I was only saving my daughter from spending eternity in hell."

"So you fed them into the chipper to save them?" Peony's voice was soft, her tactic of innocence working well.

He nodded emphatically. "Not the others, only my daughter."

"Why kill the others?" Leah asked, and received Martin's glare.

"They were corrupting my daughter," Martin said as if Leah were incredibly stupid. "I couldn't leave them alive to corrupt other women."

"Okay. You were saving your daughter. How'd you kill them?" Leah asked. *Hurry up, you crazy bastard. I want to go home.*

"It was easy. They were so stupid. What else could you expect? They were only bitches."

"Tell me how you did it, Martin," Leah told him as she tried to maintain a hold on her temper.

"I watched them all arrive. When they started that chanting shit, I went into the field and called them over to me."

"They went to you willingly?" Leah asked.

"Like sheep to the slaughter."

"Why?"

"I had hot chocolate with me."

"And?"

"And by the time I poured the last cup of hot chocolate, the first woman in line was dead. They fell like those black tiles people set up. When the first one falls over, the others fall in order. That's what those bitches did. But by the time they noticed the early ones falling, it was too late for the rest."

"What did you put in the hot chocolate?" Leah asked.

"Treebegone. The city gives me gallons of it. I keep the stuff in my truck and on the chipper."

"What is Treebegone?"

"It's stump poison," Martin told her like she was an idiot for not knowing.

"You fed tree stump poison to thirteen young women?" Peony asked incredulously.

"Yeah. Pretty clever, wasn't it? After that, it was easy. I fed those bitches into the chipper."

"How did the bishop get into the chipper?"

"After Preata killed him, he told me to put him into the chipper with the women. Then I sprayed their bits and pieces all over the field they were doing their devil worshipping in. That'll teach others not to turn away from God, and show women their places." He leaned back, looking proud, smug, and satisfied.

Leah had heard enough. She left the interrogation room followed by Peony, who looked far less enthusiastic than when they'd entered the room.

Nikki met them outside the interview room. "He's a real shit. By the way, the media's been alerted, probably by the archdiocese's attorney or one of the uniforms I sent to assist you. He'll be directing traffic at midnight in Dinali Square if I find out who he is."

"I was followed a lot during this case. I don't know if it was Grandini's people or cops. If there's a difference. Also, I'd have a good look at the commissioner. I don't know if she's in this, but something was definitely up with that. I doubt you'll find anything you can pin on her, but it's worth keeping an eye on her." Leah's phone rang. "Yeah."

"Leah, it's Scotty. I've got some good news for you."

"What's that?"

"Remember that piece of skull I told you I found?"

"Yeah."

"It definitely belonged to the bishop. I've confirmed the hole in the skull is definitely a bullet hole. Or to be precise, half a bullet hole."

"Thanks, Scotty. I think we have the gun that inflicted the hole. I'll have it sent over to ballistics for a match."

Leah turned back to Nikki.

"Scotty's found a piece of skull with a partial bullet hole in it. I told Scotty we'd send Preata's gun over to ballistics to make sure. And since Preata confessed to Quinn's murder, too, I bet the gun matches the bullet..." Leah couldn't force out the word skull. "From her case, too."

"Good. I'd love to see that arrogant asshole go all the way down," Nikki said. "You know the media outside is only the beginning of the media frenzy over this, don't you?"

"Yeah. That's why I'm going to slip out the back door." Leah didn't know where she was going to go, but she wanted to get away for a while.

"No fair. It's not nice to leave me alone with them," Nikki teased her gently.

"I'm tired and hungry, and my face is oozing. I'm leaving."

"Me, too." Peony stretched. "I can't wait to sleep in my own bed."

"All right. Leah, my offer still stands."

"I'll think about it." She had a lot to think about, but she needed space to do it.

"That's all I'm asking."

"She offered you a job here?" Peony asked.

"Yeah. You, too, if you want it."

"What'd you tell her?"

"I told her I'd think about it. This would be a good place for you to work. It's an honest shop."

"I'll think about it," Peony said with a smile.

"Call Cots and tell him to come get us," Leah said.

"He's waiting for us in the rear parking lot," Peony said. When Leah gave her a questioning look, Peony shrugged. "He said he didn't want us to have to wait around."

"I'm starved. What shall we have for dinner?" Leah asked, not wanting to talk about the case or her career or the future yet. And she didn't want to think about Quinn because her heart was breaking and her emotions were sitting close to the edge of the chasm, and she didn't want to cry until she was alone. They stopped at a diner, and it felt strange to not be looking over her shoulder or worried about being seen. Peony filled Cots in about the interviews, and he listened gravely. When she told him about Quinn's murder he looked at Leah, who shook her head to say she didn't know what it meant.

After dinner, Cots dropped Leah off at her apartment. When she walked in, the silence was overwhelming. She felt the emptiness pressing in on her. She'd been alone in the apartment when Quinn traveled on business, but then she knew Quinn would return. Now, though, she wouldn't be returning—ever. That knowledge was devastating.

She couldn't stay in the apartment where she and Quinn had lived for the five years they'd been married. She packed a bag and returned to the condo. While it, too, felt empty, it wasn't oppressive.

She took a shower and went to bed. She hoped she would get some sleep so she wouldn't have to think about what she was going to do next. *Or about Quinn.*

Chapter Twenty

The next morning, after another restless and mostly sleepless night for Leah, her team gathered in the kitchen once more. She wasn't surprised they'd come back to the condo, too. So much had happened, and she wondered if Cots felt as lost as she did. Cots fixed breakfast. As they ate, they talked about the weather.

After the breakfast dishes were put into the cleaner, they moved into the living room. "I need to tell you something. I've decided to resign from the police force," Leah said.

Cots and Peony said nothing. It was as if they couldn't decide whether they'd really heard her say she was resigning. Leah waited for them to recover their wits.

"But why, Boss?" Peony asked.

"I've put my twenty years in, for one thing. For another, it will come out that Quinn and I were married. While I've found out several more people knew about my marriage, and I didn't know they knew, they're all cops. When the public finds out about the marriage and Quinn's ties to the Grandini family, there will be a hue and cry for my head. To be honest, I don't want to face that. I just want to be left alone to deal with my grief and feelings of betrayal. I don't want to be the center of a media feeding frenzy."

"Will you regret resigning in a week?" Cots asked.

Leah smiled. "No. I've given it a lot of thought. I'm

comfortable with the decision and am even relieved to be doing it."

"Do you know what you'll be doing next?" Peony asked.

"No. I need some serious downtime to figure that out."

"When are you going to hand in your resignation?"

"Now. I'm going to deliver it to the captain's office this morning."

"Can I come with you?" Cots asked.

"Me, too," Peony said.

"You don't have to come with me. I can handle this," Leah said, incredibly touched by their show of support.

"Yeah, we know. But it would be nice to get out into the sunshine even for a little while," Peony said.

"Okay. We'll make one last field trip."

Once in the van, Cots asked, "Where do we go?"

"Good question," Leah said, not having gotten that far in her thinking. Her old captain had been killed in the bombing of the Forty-fourth and she hadn't officially been assigned a new captain. "Let's go to Nikki's precinct. I'm thinking any captain will do under the circumstances."

After she left the envelope with her resignation in it with the desk sergeant, she returned to the van feeling much lighter than when she'd entered the building. On their way back to the condo, she decided she felt like a huge burden had been lifted from her shoulders. That realization flooded her with relief. She was sure she'd made the right decision.

At the condo, they sat in the living room like they had dozens of times before. Cots looked like he had something to say but no idea how to say it.

"Just say it, Cots," Leah said.

"Quinn was working with the Grandini family. She'd been their business front for maybe six years. She didn't make any brilliant business decisions to get where she was. I mean, as it turns out, she was good at what she did, but she really got started when Stephan Grandini approached her to give the Grandini family a front person for buying property all over the city. She didn't have any qualms about working with Stephan. She bought the real estate in her own name and eventually moved it into the Grandini-owned business months later. While she was helping out the Grandini family, she was also getting wealthy herself. With Stephan's consent, of course."

"So she didn't sever her ties with the Grandinis when we met?" Leah asked. Deep down, she'd known as soon as Quinn had admitted Stephanie had a key to the apartment, but she hadn't wanted to face it.

"No. In fact, it was the old man's idea she marry you. And she continued to see Stephanie," Cots said miserably. "I'm sorry, Leah. My first obligation was to Quinn, and even after I got to know you and wanted to tell you, I couldn't. I told you as much as I could, and I felt guilty about it. But I thought you should know."

"Why are you telling her this now?" Peony asked, looking perturbed.

"She deserves to know who she was really married to, number one. The real reason Quinn wanted to keep the marriage a secret was she'd be getting information she could pass on to first Stephan, and then when he died, to Stephanie, and there would be no suspicion it was coming from Quinn. Or from you, for that matter." Cots turned his cup around and around in his hands, giving himself something to do other than look at Leah. "I think that note slipped under the door, pointing us to Grandini, was a power play. She wanted to see you face-to-face and know who her competition was, if she considered you that. She and Quinn were always playing childish games with each other." He wiped tears away with the back of his hand. "Her decision to play games in the shadows cost Quinn her life."

Leah felt hollow inside. None of it had been real. "Preata said Quinn was refusing to do what she was told. I wonder if she was trying to get out."

Cots continued turning his cup around in his hands. "I don't think we'll ever know." He looked up at Leah. "Just don't ever blame yourself. Quinn knew what she was doing, and with whom. If they ever catch Grandini, maybe you can get more answers. But if you don't, you should know I believe she did love you, in her own way."

Leah nodded but wasn't sure she agreed.

"And number two?" Peony asked. "You said number one. What's reason number two?"

He looked up. "Number two is I really enjoyed working with you both. I'd like to continue to work with you if I can. And I want to continue to see Peony."

Leah noticed Peony blushed a charming shade of pink.

"Cots, how do you know all this about Quinn?" Leah asked.

"I've known Quinn all my life. She was my sister."

"Your sister?" Peony exclaimed.

"Yeah. When Quinn decided to immigrate here, my parents were elderly. They asked her to bring me here, too, and to keep an eye on me. As usual, they got it wrong. It was me who needed to keep an eye on Quinn," Cots said. "But we never told anyone about our relationship, so it couldn't be used against us. As far as anyone knew," he smiled a little at Leah, "even you, I was just an old friend and bodyguard."

"Thanks for telling me, Cots. I thought I was only being paranoid about Quinn," Leah said.

"No. Everything you thought about her was true—the good and the bad."

Leah wasn't surprised at Cots's confession. Her gut had already told her she was right about Quinn. She'd been beating herself up about not seeing it sooner. She still couldn't believe she'd been so naïve as to believe Quinn had loved her. She reached across and touched Cots's leg. "I'm sorry you lost your sister." Their relationships with Quinn had been complicated, but that didn't mean they didn't hurt over her being gone.

"Just answer one more question for me," Leah said.

"Sure. Ask away."

"Why did you choose the name Cotsworthy when you came here?"

Peony snorted tea up her nose, and Cots looked decidedly uncomfortable.

"I didn't know a lot of English. So when we were told we'd have to choose English names, I couldn't find anything I liked. So when push came to shove I told the authorities I wanted to be called Cotsworthy because to me it sounded very British. I thought the Brits were supposed to be classier humans."

While Leah hadn't really given his name a lot of thought, she was surprised by how he had chosen it and amused no end because she'd always assumed he'd taken his time to find just the right name for himself. She sensed he wouldn't want to be teased by his lack of knowledge of his new country or laughed at, so she kept her amusement to herself.

While Cots began dismantling the murder board, Leah went to stand in front of the window. As she looked out over their street, it began snowing again. She knew her ability to trust had been severely trampled on. Only the two people in the room with her had her trust now. She squared her shoulders and turned to face them.

"Our part of the case is at an end. It's up to the attorneys now. We'll probably be called to testify, but we're officially off duty."

"What will you be doing now with all your leisure time?" Cots asked.

"Since I found out about Quinn, I don't, and won't, know who to trust. For instance, I've known Nikki since we were kids and have never questioned that she had my back, but I found myself questioning her motives yesterday. I don't want to live like that." Leah felt like her world was in free fall, a gray mass of confusion.

"I'm really sorry Quinn is responsible for your doubts and destroying your ability to trust. But I understand how it could happen," Cots said. "She was like that."

"I'm not sure I want to give Quinn that kind of credit. This has been coming for a long time. Quinn may have been a catalyst, nothing more." Though Quinn's betrayal hurt, Leah knew what she said was true.

"Sounds like you need to take some serious time off to figure out what you want," Cots said.

"I also need to deal with my feelings about Quinn. I feel like my world has been turned upside down, and I need to get it righted again before I decide what to do with the rest of my life."

"Look, I've got an idea," Peony said. "Don't laugh until you've heard me out, okay?"

Cots and Leah nodded.

"Have either of you ever been to Xing?"

Cots and Leah shook their heads.

"Let's go there, if only for a few weeks. It will get us away from all this," she said, waving her hand at the city outside the living room windows. "If nothing else, it will be warmer."

Leah didn't reject the idea out of hand. In fact, it sounded appealing. She was as tired of the frigid cold as the next person. She looked at Cots. It was obvious he was considering the offer, too.

"The flights are expensive, though." Peony winced as she said it, probably not having considered the financial part before making the suggestion.

Leah suspected the price of a ticket to Xing was prohibitively expensive and apparently not within Peony's budget.

"Let me worry about that," Leah told them.

Leah hadn't told anyone about the call she'd gotten from Quinn's attorney. He had informed her she was, thanks to Quinn, an enormously wealthy woman. Quinn had left all her considerable wealth to Leah. She'd also made two bequests— one to her long-time assistant, Klara, and one to Cots that would make him wealthy, too. She didn't know whether he'd heard from the attorney yet. She'd call the lawyer later to let him know how to get in touch with Cots.

She wasn't entirely certain about how she felt being Quinn's beneficiary. She would always wonder whether the money was obtained from the Grandini family or through legitimate means. She knew enough not to make any decisions about the money right then. She was too angry with Quinn, too betrayed by her, and still trying to piece together how she felt about her, to make any rational decisions about being her beneficiary.

"Do you think the department would let us take a vacation?" Peony asked.

"Do they have police departments on Xing?"

"A good one in Victoria where I live," Peony told her.

"How about private detectives?"

"Those, too."

"Let's go, then." Leah felt her heart lighten a little with the decision. Maybe she could start a new life on Xing. Maybe Cots and Peony would like a new start as well. She hoped so.

She could feel the depression lift just a little with the decision to leave New America. There were way too many things here to remind her of the good times with Quinn, streets they'd walked hand in hand on, restaurants they'd dined at, people they both knew. Here she only had betrayal, memories, good and bad, lost hope, and depression to look forward to. Now she'd found a scintilla of hope for a future. *Hope will be my new mantra.*

About the Author

Kay Bigelow was born in Alabama and three months later began her world travels. She has lived in Germany, Italy, Hong Kong, and much of the US. Her novels and short stories are often set in the various places she has lived. She has finally settled down (for the time being) in a small town in northern Washington State.

Books Available From Bold Strokes Books

A Country Girl's Heart by Dena Blake. When Kat Jackson gets a second chance at love, following her heart will prove the hardest decision of all. (978-1-63555-134-1)

Dangerous Waters by Radclyffe. Life, death, and war on the home front. Two women join forces against a powerful opponent, nature itself. (978-1-63555-233-1)

Fury's Death by Brey Willows. When all we hold sacred fails, who will be there to save us? (978-1-63555-063-4)

It's Not a Date by Heather Blackmore. Kade's desire to keep things with Jen on a professional level is in Jen's best interest. Yet what's in Kade's best interest…is Jen. (978-1-63555-149-5)

Killer Winter by Kay Bigelow. Just when she thought things could get no worse, homicide Lieutenant Leah Samuels learns the woman she loves has betrayed her in devastating ways. (978-1-63555-177-8)

Score by MJ Williamz. Will an addiction to pain pills destroy Ronda's chance with the woman she loves, or will she come out on top and score a happily ever after? (978-1-62639-807-8)

Spring's Wake by Aurora Rey. When wanderer Willa Lange falls for Provincetown B&B owner Nora Calhoun, will past hurts and a fifteen-year age gap keep them from finding love? (978-1-63555-035-1)

The Northwoods by Jane Hoppen. When Evelyn Bauer, disguised as her dead husband, George, travels to a Northwoods logging camp to work, she and the camp cook Sarah Bell forge a friendship fraught with both tenderness and turmoil. (978-1-63555-143-3)

Truth or Dare by C. Spencer. For a group of six lesbian friends, life changes course after one long snow-filled weekend. (978-1-63555-148-8)

A Heart to Call Home by Jeannie Levig. When Jessie Weldon returns to her hometown after thirty years, can she and her childhood crush Dakota Scott heal the tragic past that links them? (978-1-63555-059-7)

Children of the Healer by Barbara Ann Wright. Life becomes desperate for ex-soldier Cordelia Ross when the indigenous aliens of her planet are drawn into a civil war and old enemies linger in the shadows. Book Three of the Godfall Series. (978-1-63555-031-3)

Hearts Like Hers by Melissa Brayden. Coffee shop owner Autumn Primm is ready to cut loose and live a little, but is the baggage that comes with out-of-towner Kate Carpenter too heavy for anything long term? (978-1-63555-014-6)

Love at Cooper's Creek by Missouri Vaun. Shaw Daily flees corporate life to find solace in the rural Blue Ridge Mountains, but escapism eludes her when her attentions are captured by small town beauty Kate Elkins. (978-1-62639-960-0)

Twice in a Lifetime by PJ Trebelhorn. Detective Callie Burke can't deny the growing attraction to her late friend's widow, Taylor Fletcher, who also happens to own the bar where Callie's sister works. (978-1-63555-033-7)

Undiscovered Affinity by Jane Hardee. Will a no-strings-attached affair be enough to break Olivia's control and convince Cardic that love does exist? (978-1-63555-061-0)

Between Sand and Stardust by Tina Michele. Are the lifelong bonds of love strong enough to conquer time, distance, and heartache when Haven Thorne and Willa Bennette are given another chance at forever? (978-1-62639-940-2)

Charming the Vicar by Jenny Frame. When magician and atheist Finn Kane seeks refuge in an English village after a spiritual crisis, can local vicar Bridget Claremont restore her faith in life and love? (978-1-63555-029-0)

Data Capture by Jesse J. Thoma. Lola Walker is undercover on the hunt for cybercriminals while trying not to notice the woman who might be perfectly wrong for her for all the right reasons. (978-1-62639-985-3)

Epicurean Delights by Renee Roman. Ariana Marks had no idea a leisure swim would lead to being rescued, in more ways than one, by the charismatic Hudson Frost. (978-1-63555-100-6)

Heart of the Devil by Ali Vali. We know most of Cain and Emma Casey's story, but Heart of the Devil will take you back to where it began one fateful night with a tray loaded with beer. (978-1-63555-045-0)

Known Threat by Kara A. McLeod. When Special Agent Ryan O'Connor reluctantly questions who protects the Secret Service, she learns courage truly is found in unlikely places. Agent O'Connor Series #3 (978-1-63555-132-7)

Seer and the Shield by D. Jackson Leigh. Time is running out for the Dragon Horse Army while two unlikely heroines struggle to put aside their attraction and find a way to stop a deadly cult. Dragon Horse War, Book 3 (978-1-63555-170-9)

The Universe Between Us by Jane C. Esther. Ana Mitchell must make the hardest choice of her life: the promise of new love Jolie Dann on Earth, or a humanity-saving mission to colonize Mars. (978-1-63555-106-8)

Touch by Kris Bryant. Can one touch heal a heart? (978-1-63555-084-9)

A More Perfect Union by Carsen Taite. Major Zoey Granger and DC fixer Rook Daniels risk their reputations for a chance at true love while dealing with a scandal that threatens to rock the military. (978-1-62639-754-5)

Arrival by Gun Brooke. The spaceship *Pathfinder* reaches its passengers' new homeworld where danger lurks in the shadows while Pamas Seclan disembarks and finds unexpected love in young science genius Darmiya Do Voy. (978-1-62639-859-7)

Captain's Choice by VK Powell. Architect Kerstin Anthony's life is going to plan until Bennett Carlyle, the first girl she ever kissed, is assigned to her latest and most important project, a police district substation. (978-1-62639-997-6)

Falling Into Her by Erin Zak. Pam Phillips, widow at the age of forty, meets Kathryn Hawthorne, local Chicago celebrity, and it changes her life forever—in ways she hadn't even considered possible. (978-1-63555-092-4)

Hookin' Up by MJ Williamz. Will Leah get what she needs from casual hookups or will she see the love she desires right in front of her? (978-1-63555-051-1)

King of Thieves by Shea Godfrey. When art thief Casey Marinos meets bounty hunter Finnegan Starkweather, the crimes of the past just might set the stage for a payoff worth more than she ever dreamed possible. (978-1-63555-007-8)

Lucy's Chance by Jackie D. As a serial killer haunts the streets, Lucy tries to stitch up old wounds with her first love in the wake of a small town's rapid descent into chaos. (978-1-63555-027-6)

Right Here, Right Now by Georgia Beers. When Alicia Wright moves into the office next door to Lacey Chamberlain's accounting firm, Lacey is about to find out that sometimes the last person you want is exactly the person you need. (978-1-63555-154-9)

Strictly Need to Know by MB Austin. Covert operator Maji Rios will do whatever she must to complete her mission, but saving a gorgeous stranger from Russian mobsters was not in her plans. (978-1-63555-114-3)

Tailor-Made by Yolanda Wallace. Tailor Grace Henderson doesn't date clients, but when she meets gender-bending model Dakota Lane, she's tempted to throw all the rules out the window. (978-1-63555-081-8)

Time Will Tell by M. Ullrich. With the ability to time travel, Eva Caldwell will have to decide between having it all and erasing it all. (978-1-63555-088-7)

Change in Time by Robyn Nyx. Working in the past is hell on your future. The Extractor series: Book Two. (978-1-62639-880-1)

Love After Hours by Radclyffe. When Gina Antonelli agrees to renovate Carrie Longmire's new house, she doesn't welcome Carrie's overtures at friendship or her own unexpected attraction. A Rivers Community Novel. (978-1-63555-090-0)

Nantucket Rose by CF Frizzell. Maggie Jordan can't wait to convert a historic Nantucket home into a B&B, but doesn't expect to fall for mariner Ellis Chilton, who has more claim to the house than Maggie realizes. (978-1-63555-056-6)

Picture Perfect by Lisa Moreau. Falling in love wasn't supposed to be part of the stakes for Olive and Gabby, rival photographers in the competition of a lifetime. (978-1-62639-975-4)

Set the Stage by Karis Walsh. Actress Emilie Danvers takes the stage again in Ashland, Oregon, little realizing that landscaper Arden Philips is about to offer her a very personal romantic lead role. (978-1-63555-087-0)

Strike a Match by Fiona Riley. When their attempts at matchmaking fizzle out, firefighter Sasha and reluctant millionairess Abby find themselves turning to each other to strike a perfect match. (978-1-62639-999-0)

The Price of Cash by Ashley Bartlett. Cash Braddock is doing her best to keep her business afloat, stay out of jail, and avoid Detective Kallen. It's not working. (978-1-62639-708-8)

Captured Soul by Laydin Michaels. Can Kadence Munroe save the woman she loves from a twisted killer, or will she lose her to a collector of souls? (978-1-62639-915-0)

Under Her Wing by Ronica Black. At Angel's Wings Rescue, dogs are usually the ones saved, but when quiet Kassandra Haden meets outspoken owner Jayden Beaumont, the two stubborn women just might end up saving each other. (978-1-63555-077-1)